MW01152346

NONVERBAL

Peggy Moffitt Earnest

Text: © 2019 Margaret (Peggy) M. Earnest

Cover Photography: ©2019 Margaret (Peggy) M. Earnest

No part of this publication shall be reproduced, distributed or stored without the written permission of the author.

This book is dedicated, with deep admiration, to the families of nonverbal children and especially those who have directly touched my life. You are an invaluable resource in sharing their stories with the world.

Table of Contents

Prologue

"STUPID! STUPID! STUPID!" Susan screamed over and over again through her tears. Thank God for the solace of her car. It was the first time she'd had one second alone in the past two weeks of hell. That was far too long to hold all of this anger and heartbreak inside, but she had to do it. For the kids. Always for the kids.

Even now, on the way to work, she couldn't let it all out. She couldn't risk collapsing from emotional exhaustion in the middle of the floor once she got to the hospital. Nor could she show up all bleary eyed and puffy; it would scare the *other* kids, her patients. She would allow herself another few minutes of self-pity, and then she would pull herself together and paint a smile on her face.

Susan took a deep breath and felt her mind go easily to the place it had gone a thousand times already. Even though she hadn't been able to outwardly vent her feelings, she had been perfectly free to beat herself up internally for fourteen days straight. *Why didn't I check?* she thought. There had been no time in the hustle of packing for the long weekend. She'd just trusted that Jake would do as she asked, and he had, in his own way.

Why didn't I specifically tell him to use the new one? she thought. Jake's iPad was almost as necessary as food and air in his world. He used it, along with gestures, signs, and his versions of "words" to communicate with anyone and everyone who would listen and even some who weren't interested in listening. Even bigger than communicating, though, was the music. Jake *loved* to play music, whether straight songs through his headphones or YouTube videos of his favorite "bands," which included Sesame Street and the Dreamtime Dudes. Jake just called them "bah" and "doo," respectively. At fifteen years old, Jake could say about fifty approximations of words, but the words came *only* if two very specific stipulations were met. First, although he used words to communicate what he needed, Jake rarely actually said the words—he sang them. Second, the only words Jake had ever learned to sing were words he learned from Big Bird or the "Dudes" or other songs they had concocted for specific purposes when he was little. It made life interesting until you learned his rules, but in their house it was automatic: If you wanted Jake to speak, you sang to him. If you wanted to stop singing and get something else done for a moment, you made sure the iPad was charged.

When she got the phone call on the first night of camp, she had realized with absolute horror that she hadn't specifically told Jake

2

to use the new charger for his iPad. Instead, she'd made the fatal mistake of assuming that Jake knew. That was the problem, though; she could never assume that Jake was able to process what was said to him in the same way that Emily or anyone else did. Jake understood the facts. He understood the concrete and the routine. He did not understand the implied. That, in a nutshell, was why their house had burned to the ground.

Jake's old charger had gotten stuck in the zipper of his backpack one too many times. It was frayed and rarely worked effectively unless you were able to jiggle it into submission. The day before the fire, she and Jake had made a special trip to Target for "camp" supplies and a new iPad charger. That charger, unfortunately, was never used. *If only I had said* one *more word. If only I had said, "Charge your iPad with the* new *charger,"* Susan thought, *things would be looking a lot better right now.*

The day of the fire, Jake grabbed his iPad off the charger, and their small family had taken off for their annual three-day weekend at Camp Blue Skies in Rhode Island. Susan, Jake, and his seventeen-year-old sister, Emily, had all been looking forward to the trip, each for their own reasons. Jake loved the beach, the music, the endless, accessible activities that remained the same every year, and the people. Those

3

people had grown to love and *understand* him over the past twelve years of camps. Susan, for her part, was looking forward to spending time with the parents and maybe sneaking a bottle or two of wine onto the beach. It was the one time during the year that she felt that she didn't have to explain what it was like to be the parent of a special needs child. Everyone there was in the same boat, and there was an inherent, almost telepathic, understanding among each and every family that attended Blue Skies each summer. Even Emily had no complaints. For her, it was a well-deserved change of pace, a respite from caretaking, and a place where she could connect with the many others siblings over beach time and bonfires.

But this year, the mood changed suddenly and dramatically when the fire chief tracked Susan down at 2:00 a.m., waking her from a sound sleep to deliver the news. She had raced the two hours home to Connecticut, leaving the kids in the care of camp friends rather than opting to wake them up. She did not want them to witness the fire that was devouring life as they knew it. It was a good call, too, because the nightmare of what she'd seen would live in Susan's memory for the rest of her life.

Fast-forward two weeks, and the fire was still being investigated. Until the report was finalized, there would be no insurance money, so for now, they were shacking up at Bridget's house and surviving on community donations, some of which were more welcome than others.

Chapter 1

Home

Once a big sister...always a big sister. Bridget couldn't help but feel protective of her little sister all the time—it was in her blood. Watching out for Susan had been her job ever since the little pink bundle of joy came home on Bridget's own third birthday, but this time, there was no protecting her. The damage was already done.

They had stayed through the wee hours of the morning and into the next day, watching in disbelief. Even though Bridget could feel the intense heat of the blaze on her face, she still could not believe this was Susan's house. Even though she could see the reflection of the red-orange emergency lights flashing across her sister's tear-streaked face, even though she could taste the thick smoke in her throat, and even though she saw the walls of her sister's home burning and crumbling one by one, she could not convince herself that it was happening. It was like watching a slow-motion horror movie. It seemed beyond reason that her beautiful sister could be the victim of such a cruel twist of fate.

Seriously, what had Susan done to deserve this? Nothing but work hard and support her children. Nothing but remain a rock for the two greatest gifts life had blessed her with. Susan was the strongest and most resilient person that Bridget had ever met. She'd had cancer as a child, but she fought and recovered and even started to thrive by the time she got to high school. She met Patrick in the twelfth grade and dated him faithfully through college and graduate school. They married as soon as Patrick got out of grad school and started a family right away. Emily came first, and two years later, Jake was born.

Then, two words changed Susan's life once again. When the doctor said, "Down syndrome," Patrick disappeared. He didn't physically leave, but he seemed to check out emotionally at that very moment. He became detached, almost robotic in his fathering of both kids. He was cold and sullen and would withdraw from Susan's touch. From that time on, Bridget vowed to step up and provide support for her sister, her niece, and her newborn nephew. If Patrick had stuck around, he would have been in for the most joyous and unexpected ride of his life.

It took Patrick about six months to finally pack up his things and move out. By then, he had become somewhat of a ghost and, surprisingly, Susan took his departure in stride. Things seemed to reach a new level of peacefulness in their little house after he left. Jake had been discharged from the NICU, and two of his three heart surgeries were behind him. He began to eat well and gain strength. Best of all, he began to come to life. To this day, Jake could charm the pants off anybody he met with his upbeat personality and that ridiculously happy smile.

Susan, for her part, just kept marching forward with a new kind of normalcy. Bridget admired her ability to accept what life handed her and to live in the moment. She watched as her sister tirelessly researched treatments and therapies and applied only those that she thought were right for their family and for Jake's future. Susan always said that Jake was born to be what he was meant to be and that her job was not to find ways to change him but to just enjoy him. Though Susan was Bridget's little sister, she was also her biggest inspiration.

So, no, Bridget could not think of a single solitary reason why God would send this hardship on her sister. She said a silent prayer that the fire would not break her sister's spirit, but she knew that her strength would be tested further. The fire was contained, the future was unsure, but the worst was yet to come. Susan still had to tell her kids.

The kids arrived at what was left of their home at around noon that day with some old friends from camp. Susan intercepted them at the end of the long driveway to break the news, knowing that it would take a long time to sink in for all of them, but especially for Jake. As soon as Susan managed to choke out the awful news, Emily ran down the gravel driveway to where the house had stood just yesterday. Jake trailed behind at a considerable distance, both because Emily was so fast and because Jake was not a fan of running unless it was for a very good reason. Emily stopped short when the house came into view and breathlessly whispered, "How could this have happened?"

Jake trotted up about a full minute later. Bridget carefully watched his face. Up until now, his life was based on routines and predictability. If something novel was going on, either Susan or one of Jake's teachers would prepare him ahead of time using a social story so he could visually understand what was going to happen. What happened if the event was completely unscripted, unplanned, and beyond comprehension? Bridget waited anxiously to find out.

Emily had fallen to her knees and begun to cry softly, but she knew by the cadence of his steps that Jake was approaching and automatically reached her hand upward and toward him. Bridget expected that Jake would fall into Emily's gesture, kneel down beside her, lift a strand of her hair between his thumb and forefinger, and begin to rub it. This simple act was one that he had been doing since he was a baby in her arms, and it was always comforting for both of them.

To Bridget's surprise, that was not what Jake did. Instead, he threw his iPad to the ground and took off running. Bridget watched with horror and amazement as Jake disappeared quickly into the woods. "Damnit," she muttered as she momentarily debated what she should do. A quick scan of her surroundings told her that Susan was deep in conversation with the fire chief and Emily was far too distraught to be burdened any further at the moment. So Bridget picked up the iPad and followed Jake into the shade of the woods.

She was surprised that she could not find Jake right away and grateful when she discovered that there was a rough path that cut through the woods. She trotted along the trail, wearing the flimsy cotton pajama pants and white T-shirt that she always slept in. Bridget was silently thankful that she'd had the foresight to at least put on a bra and some sneakers when Susan had called her in the middle of the night and told her about the fire. She called Jake's name over and over again with as much calmness as she could muster.

It felt as though she had been running for hours when she came to a clearing in the woods that led to the quiet road. The midday summer sunlight blinded her briefly when she stepped out onto the road, but she could faintly make out two figures running toward her. By the gait, she ascertained that one was Jake, and she let out a sigh of relief. The other figure also tried to run, but never so fast that they left Jake behind. The person held a large object in one hand, and it swung wildly back and forth as they moved. In silhouette, it looked like a tennis racquet or a large fishing net. Bridget could not quite make out what it was.

As the pair got closer, Bridget heard the sound of two familiar voices: Jake's and Peter's. She was truly taken aback that Jake's immediate reaction after seeing their home was to take off and run three-quarters of a mile to Peter's house.

"Bridget, what's happening?" Peter asked breathlessly. He looked rough, as if he had just awoken from a deep sleep. His dark hair, which he usually kept straight and neat, fanned out like a peacock's feathers in every direction, and his glasses were not quite on his nose. Yet he had grabbed his guitar on the way out the door. That just didn't seem to be a necessity right now. Bridget felt as if she was walking around in a strange dream.

Peter saw the unmistakable look of confusion on Bridget's face and quickly tried to clarify by explaining, "Jake told me to bring this, and he seemed desperate to say something." Bridget immediately understood.

Peter was a classmate of Emily's and had been the Prescotts' neighbor for the past fifteen years. He and Emily used to run around in diapers together when they were younger, though discussing that now that they were teens was definitely off limits. Throughout those years, Peter had grown to love and understand Jake as almost nobody, besides his family, did. Three times a week, he came over to hang out with Jake, play the guitar, and sing songs. They were Dudes songs mostly, but Peter often tried to add slight variations to the tunes or the lyrics to see if he could get Jake to say some new words. Peter had not been scheduled for one of their sessions today, nor was he aware of what had been happening at the Prescotts' for the past twelve hours, so Bridget wearily broke the awful news to him. She could see his big, deep-green eyes slowly filling with tears as she spoke, and it broke her heart to have to tell him. Though he didn't live there, he had spent more than enough time with them to make many happy memories in that house too.

Jake was obviously exhausted from his sprint to Peter's house, so they continued back toward the Prescotts' house at a slower pace. Peter held Jake's hand as they walked, and nobody said a word. There was really nothing to say that would change things. They emerged from the woods and onto Jake's driveway. Susan and Emily were still on their knees, looking distraught and broken. Bridget walked away for a few moments to collect her thoughts and make some phone calls. Peter put his guitar down, knelt down beside the women, put his arms around them, and spoke softly to them as he took in the horrific scene.

Jake suddenly sprinted in Bridget's direction. He lunged quickly at her, stumbling a bit in his fatigue, and grabbed his iPad, which she had forgotten she was still holding. He ran back and pulled Peter to his feet rather harshly. All of this was completely out of character for the generally laid-back Jake. He led Peter desperately over to his guitar, which rested in the grass at the edge of the path. Jake found the word "home" on his iPad, which, thankfully, still worked even after being thrown to the ground.

Peter cast a bewildered and uncomfortable glance in Emily and Susan's direction. Not a word needed to pass between them for Susan to understand, and she responded by saying, "Go ahead, Peter." They all knew that when Jake wanted to say something, he could not move on until it was said. Music coaxed the words out, and Peter possessed the music. He looked awkwardly self-aware and totally out of place as he picked up his guitar and began to strum the tune. He had sung this with Jake at least a thousand times before, but it seemed completely inappropriate at this moment.

"Really, Peter, it's OK," Susan said. "Keep going. It will help Jake."

With that, Peter and Jake sang "Home," by the Dreamtime Dudes. It was a song that Jake sang anytime he wanted to go home, but going home was not an option anymore.

It's your place
It's my place
It's her place
It's our place
Yeah, this is the best place
Because it's my home

I play here
I eat here
I lay down
To sleep here
Yeah, this is the best place
Because it's my home

Peter sang, weakly at first, with Jake filling in the word "home" at every opportunity. Each time Peter came to the end of the song, Jake would tug on his shirt and sign "more" so that Peter would begin again. Nobody was sure what Jake was truly trying to communicate about his home. Nobody was sure of anything except the intricate complexities that were unique to Jake's own mind.

After the fourth or fifth rendition, Emily and Susan joined the boys, and the song gained energy and strength as it carried over the trees and into the bright summer sky. When Bridget walked back toward them, she was unexpectedly amused by the irony of the scene that played out before her. Three grown people and one very large dancing child, singing a children's tune not around a campfire but around the smoldering embers of what used to be their home. This was an image she would not soon forget, and as she watched them, Bridget was overcome by the unshakable feeling that, somehow, everything would eventually be all right.

Chapter 2

Hug

"Damn fire!" Emily grumbled as she fidgeted in front of the full-length mirror in her room at Aunt Bridget's house. The clothes that had been donated were cheap and ill fitting, and since Emily had lost some weight over the past two weeks, they were extremely uncomfortable. As she scowled at herself in the plaid skirt and itchy, white, short-sleeved shirt, she longed for the endless piles of brand-name clothing and perfectly broken-in jeans that were now just dust and ashes under the burnt beams of their house.

Mom had promised to take her shopping as soon as she got her paycheck today. The timing of that paycheck royally sucked, though, because now Emily had to wear charity clothes on her first day of school. She had never felt so uncomfortable in her life, and she was seriously ticked off about that and a million other things. Her whole life, she had dreamed about what her senior year of high school would be like. It would be perfection to be at the top of the food chain, popular, athletic, and almost free of school. In a word: bliss. The fire had changed everything about that dream.

They had lost literally everything that they owned in the stupid, senseless fire. Emily knew her peers often used the word "literally" to mean the exact opposite of what it really meant. Like when her best friend, Sophie, said, "Did you see how tall Hannah got over the summer? She is literally the size of a giraffe." But in this case, Emily used "literally" in its purest and most precise form. The family lost all of their earthly belongings, with the exception of what they had packed for their trip, and all that remained of the house was the deep pit of the basement, filled with charred memories. For the past two weeks, the Prescotts had been surviving, for the most part, on the kindness of others. Clothing drives and fundraisers had sprung up on their behalf before the fire was even completely out. They received enough money to rent a small car and to buy some groceries and necessary school supplies. There wasn't enough money for clothing quite yet, and with her dad out of the country on business, Emily couldn't even hit him up.

In Emily's opinion, another major problem was that the fire had drawn a lot of local and statewide news coverage. Stories ran in every media outlet imaginable and from every different angle those know-it-all reporters could uncover. The headlines ranged from "Family of Special Needs Child Loses Everything" to "Catastrophe Strikes for High School Cross-Country Star." Emily had lost her things, but she'd also lost her personal anonymity, and it made her feel completely exposed. All she wanted was to be a normal seventeen-year-old at the beginning of the end of her high school journey. To go through a disaster of this magnitude once was a nightmare, but every time someone acted concerned, asked questions, or showed pity, Emily felt like she was reliving the whole thing. She did not want to be reminded that they were suddenly penniless and virtually homeless. A week ago, it all got to be too overwhelming for her, so she decided to do her best to ignore the whole thing for a while. She stopped reading the paper and watching TV. She closed all of her social media accounts and only texted or called the people she wanted to talk to, like Nat and Sophie. Life was surprisingly peaceful without the constant buzz of social media, and the quiet allowed her to pretend that she was just visiting Aunt Bridget for a few nights.

Stranding herself on an island of limited technology had given her a short respite, but today she would have to face the music. There was no unplugging from real-life teenage curiosity, and because of the fire, there would be a lot of fresh gossip when Emily entered Brighton Regional this morning. It would start with everyone watching her as she walked Jake to room 64. Normally, it was Mom's job to get Jake to his first day of school, but she was picking up as many extra shifts as she could because they needed the money, so she had been at work for several hours already. Aunt Bridget's house was out of district, and the school couldn't bus Jake to school either. Jake's transportation and safe delivery to school was up to Emily for the foreseeable future. As she and Jake climbed into her mom's bright orange Jeep and headed for school, Emily's insides churned with a nausea-inducing mixture of anger and anxiety. She could not get comfortable in her own skin. Or her charity clothes.

They parked the Jeep in Emily's assigned spot and headed for the side door, Emily holding Jake's hand, keeping him safe as they walked through the busy parking lot. Just as they pushed through the heavy glass door, Emily felt an arm draped around her shoulder and a warm, welcome presence from behind her. Warren Jepson wrapped Emily and Jake all too briefly in his long, muscular arms and shouted, "First senior selfie!" He snapped a shot of the three of them before Emily had a chance to even look up and smile. Warren took off as quickly as he had approached them, but Emily could still feel the tingling around her shoulders where he had touched her. She quietly sighed and let a vision of Warren's flawless face slip into her mind for a blissful moment. A face like that could make her forget all her troubles.

Jake brought her back to reality.

Sweet Jake. He could be as embarrassing as he was amazing sometimes.

Unlike Emily, Jake relished the clothing donations that had come his way. He was especially proud of the new shirts that hung in his closet...the Elmos, the Ernies, the Big Birds, and even one or two Dreamtime Dudes concert tees. Often, Jake couldn't see the forest for the trees. The kid hadn't skipped a beat since the day after the fire; he was too excited about living with Aunt Bridget, playing with her dogs, and wearing his new shirts to his new school. Plus, the single possession that had survived the fire was his precious iPad, since it had been in the Jeep when it happened. Emily felt a mild twinge of jealousy at his overall lack of awareness. He was the very definition of "ignorance is bliss," which, she now realized, was not a bad thing sometimes.

Jake was not a shy young man, and though it was his first day of high school, in his mind, he was already the king. After Warren jogged away, it took them ten minutes to walk the thirty seconds to the resource room while, wordlessly, Jake tapped random strangers on the shoulder and presented his shirt to them. Today, he had chosen a

Cookie Monster shirt and had been grinning ear to ear ever since he put it on before breakfast.

Most of Emily's friends would have expected Jake's interruption and taken it in stride, but the kids in this hallway looked pretty unfamiliar, probably because they were mostly freshmen from the three different towns that Brighton Regional High School served. Jake's classmates, at least for the next four years, greeted him with a variety of reactions, and Emily couldn't ascertain which kids already knew him and which were meeting him for the first time.

One by one, he zoned in on classmates and tapped them silently on the shoulder. There was no rhyme or reason to who was chosen and who was not, at least from Emily's point of view. With a giant grin and the look of unmistakable pride on his face, Jake stretched out the front of his shirt and said, "Da daaaaaaaa!" (It was his version of "Ta-da!".) Some of the kids gave him a quizzical look, some rolled their eyes, and some ignored him completely, which was something Jake didn't understand. He took that as an invitation to persist until they responded.

One or two of the kids were pleasant enough to give him a thumbs-up or a fist bump before moving along.

When they finally reached the door to room 64, Emily was beginning to think that she might actually make it to her first class on time...until Jake made a beeline to one final classmate. Emily had never seen her before. She was sitting with her knees up almost to her chin in the small corner between the hallway and the door to room 64. Even though it was August 28 and about ninety degrees in the school, she wore a gray knit hat that covered the top of her head and forehead. Her face was tilted down toward the small pad she held on her lap and on which she was scribbling intensely. Emily couldn't tell what she looked like because her long, wavy blond hair cascaded down over the rest of her downcast face.

Jake tapped her on her knit cap and presented his shirt with his traditional excitement. The girl didn't move. She just said, "Go to hell," and kept scribbling.

Surprisingly, Jake seemed to take the hint this time and turned toward the door of room 64. Emily felt prematurely relieved until he pulled out his talker and found a single word: hug. Her heart sank. That meant Jake wanted to say "hug," and in order to say it, Emily would have to sing him the song.

"Oh, Jake," Emily said more quietly and patiently than she felt. "OK, bud."

She'd had a feeling this might happen but had prayed it would not. It was the first day of her senior year, but it was his first-ever day of high school. Emily did not want to be the single person who was responsible for setting him off before the first bell rang on the first day of school.

She rifled through her memory and pulled out the familiar song that Jake wanted to sing...

right now...

in the middle of a hallway...

filled with dozens of kids...

on the first, albeit incredibly awkward, day of her senior year.

Emily took a deep breath and forced herself to get it over with.

> *Put your hand out ONE*
> *Put your hand out TWO*
> *Give a hug to me and*
> *I'll give a hug to you*

AND THEN A KIIIIIIIIIIIISSSSSS

Jake happily filled in the words "hug...me," "hug...you," and "KISS" in his best imitation of Eric, the Dude with the incredibly baritone voice. Then he hugged Emily, gave her a long kiss, and skipped into room 64.

Emily thought she heard Gray Hat snort and say something like, "How tender," under her breath, but she couldn't be sure. She booked it out of there as soon as the last note was done.

Chapter 3

Gray Hat

Emily had already settled in her seat and taken out a crisp new notebook and pencil when Mr. Clarkson walked over and tapped on her desk. She looked up in response as he handed her a pink note and whispered, "I'm so sorry about the fire." Emily was accustomed to a constant scowl on Mr. Clarkson's face, and she found his look of clear empathy a little disconcerting. She was surprised when she felt a lump rising in her throat. It was the first of many times she would have to swallow it back throughout the coming days.

Emily opened the note and was greeted with a request to visit Mr. Grant, the new school psychologist, at her earliest convenience. *Gee*, Emily thought sarcastically, *I wonder what this could be about.* It would honestly be nice just to get through her first day without having the fire, and her reaction to it, psychoanalyzed by anyone. Apparently, nobody cared about making her first day as normal as possible.

Emily got through English and trig before she had a free block, and then she headed down to the office to get the "meeting" over with. The office was so crowded that she had to squeeze into a small spot by the door just to find a place to wait. Brighton was a fairly large school, and it looked as if there were a lot of new students in the office dealing with beginning-of-the-year formalities. Hopefully she could get this over with and get back to senior study hall in time to catch up on some of the summer gossip with Soph and a few of their other friends.

Rather than having the secretary formally call her in, Mr. Grant came out of his office to find Emily himself. Emily was not sure how he knew who she was, but he did. He came right over to her and said, "Emily, it's a pleasure to meet you. I'm Mr. Grant. I've taken over for Mrs. Shannon, who, as you know, retired at the end of last year."

Mr. Grant was younger than Emily had imagined, maybe in his late twenties or early thirties. He had dirty-blond hair that he swooped toward the left side of his head in a preppy sort of way. He had kind, light brown eyes, and a large, goofy smile. "Shall we?" he said, gesturing toward the hallway to his office. Emily nodded and followed.

Emily was surprised that she felt instantly comfortable with Mr. Grant, not at all like Mrs. Shannon. Whenever Emily had come to talk to Mrs. Shannon, she had always questioned whether it was worth the trouble. Emily had always felt judged and on edge in Mrs.

Shannon's presence. Sometimes she even left there feeling more stressed out than when she went in.

When they reached the office, Mr. Grant closed the door behind them and extended a hand toward one of the two gray-fabric chairs that faced his desk, and Emily dutifully sat down. The décor had not changed a bit, but Emily felt much more relaxed than she ever had sitting in this chair. Mr. Grant was searching for something on his disaster of a desk, so Emily looked around to see if he had added any personal touches to the office.

Even though the state of his desk and the brown, cardboard boxes on the floor told her that he hadn't completely settled into his new job, she did notice that he had taken the time to put two photos on his desk and a few on his wall. The photos on his desk, along with a quick glance at his left ring finger, told her that he was married to a tiny strawberry blonde with a beautiful smile, and that they had a baby. Based on the Red Sox outfit and mini bat that rested beside the baby in the photo, Emily deduced it was a boy. Mr. Grant smiled when he saw Emily's eyes resting on the photo. "That's Christopher," he said proudly, "my seven-month-old insomniac. In case you were wondering where the giant bags under my eyes come from, he's the culprit."

Emily laughed and thought, *Just when you think his grin can't get any goofier, it does.* It was kind of adorable.

Mr. Grant apologized for taking up her time and continued to search for the hopelessly lost item on his desk. Emily's eyes lifted from Christopher to the photos on the wall. Emily was confused by what these other photos said about Mr. Grant. There was another picture of a young child, this time a smiling little pony-tailed girl in a frame on the wall, between two other photos. The girl looked to be about seven or eight years old, with red hair, deep brown eyes, and a familiar goofy smile. She had freckles all over her face. To the left of her picture was a photo of an empty playground. To the right was a close-up of a small boulder with an engraved sign on it. From her vantage point, Emily could not make out what the sign said, nor did she have much more time to consider why the girl's photo was not on the desk, next to Christopher's. She was obviously Mr. Grant's daughter.

"All set," Mr. Grant said, interrupting her thoughts. "Now, let's get on with this so you can get out of here in time for study hall." Emily realized that Mr. Grant had been looking for a copy of her schedule, which she already had right on top of her notebook if he had just asked. Emily gave him an impatient look and decided to cut him off before he even had the time to ask about the fire.

"Mr. Grant," she said, "this is the first day of senior year. For so many reasons, it is already off to a crappy start, so if you're planning on making me talk about the fire or my feelings about it, I just want to stop you before you even get started. The last thing I need is to rehash the gory details and risk breaking into tears within ten minutes of meeting you." Emily really was afraid she would start crying, but she wasn't at all concerned about Mr. Grant's first impression. Warren was in her next class, and having running mascara all over her face when she saw him was just not an option.

"Direct," Mr. Grant said, not even bothering to hide his grin. "I like that a lot, and I think we'll get along well if you continue to share exactly what and how you are feeling. I didn't necessarily call you down here to rehash those events, at least not now. I called you here mainly to introduce myself and to see if there is anything that you need from me. Beyond that, I would like you to remember two things. One, I think that at some point, you will need to discuss your feelings with someone who is qualified to handle it. That would be me. Two, you might also like to talk with someone who has also been through tragic events and lived to tell about it." He raised his hand slightly in the air and said, "That would be me again. We don't need to exchange details today. Just know that I am here to support you. If you want to chat about Jake, we can talk about Jake; if you want to talk about the impact of the fire on everything around you, we can tackle that as well…when the time is right. There will be a day when you can't bury your feelings anymore, and from experience, I can tell you that your friends won't ever be able to completely understand your loss. I hope you see me as an ally in this awful hand you've been dealt. I am positive you will need one. I am just not sure exactly when."

Emily realized the damn lump was back in her throat again, and this time it was bigger than before. "OK, thanks," she managed to choke out. "I will definitely keep that in mind."

She collected her things, exchanged "nice to meet you" pleasantries with Mr. Grant, and walked out of his office with a sigh of relief and her mascara intact. But she sensed that he was right behind her. For a split second, she thought about turning around and reiterating that she was not in the mood to discuss the situation further. Then she heard him stop to introduce himself again, this time to Gray Hat, who was waiting in the main office. "Julie Wallace?" he said as he stuck his hand out to shake hers. Gray Hat nodded. "I'm Mr. Grant. It's a pleasure to meet you. Please, follow me."

Emily's mouth dropped open as she finally got a good look at Gray Hat's face. *Julie Wallace is back?* she thought. *Unbelievable.*

Chapter 4

Beautiful Me

Peter belted out his current favorite song as the wind blew his hair and the sun warmed his face. Even though his car was older than dirt and a broken-down piece of junk, it was a broken-down piece of *convertible* junk. For that, and his amazing speaker system, Peter was always grateful on days like this. The first day of school was over, the rest of his senior year was ahead of him, and he was looking forward to a relaxing ride. Usually, Peter grabbed his guitar and a quick snack before heading through the woods to Jake's house for their after-school sessions. Until Jake's house was rebuilt, it was going to take some extra time to get to him each day. Peter was shuffling a country music mix that always made him smile from ear to ear. Maybe he could try to teach Jake a little "Chicken Fried" today. The thought made him chuckle.

He pulled up to Bridget's house about twenty minutes later, still in a stellar mood, and knocked on the door. Peter heard the dogs barking and expected to see Bridget on the other side of door when it opened. Instead, he was greeted by Emily wearing a pair of blue running shorts and an orange tank top. Peter blushed a little and stammered, "H-hey, Emily" as he tried to focus on her eyes. "I didn't expect to see you here today." Emily was rarely home after school because of her intensive training and social schedules.

"Hey, Peter," Emily said. "There's no cross-country practice for the first couple days of school. Plus somebody has to give Jake a ride home until we get everything figured out. Now that you're here, I'm heading out for a run. Jake is in the kitchen having a snack. See you in a little bit."

Emily headed out the door in a sprint, and Peter took a moment to watch her lean, graceful legs as she went. His already great mood improved even more.

Having never been here, Peter wasn't familiar with Bridget's house, and it took him a minute or two to find Jake. When he entered the kitchen, he saw Jake sitting, with his back toward Peter, at the breakfast bar. Jake didn't notice him at first because he was busy making mini sandwiches out of an assortment of cheese crackers, jelly beans, and marshmallows. Peter made a mental note to have him dance out his energy before the sugar crash.

"Hey, Jake," Peter said as he touched him firmly on the shoulder.

"Mamama," Jake mumbled in response, his mouth full of cheese cracker sandwiches. He smiled through the orange crumbs and pushed one of his creations toward Peter, offering him the treat. Peter gladly obliged and popped it into his mouth with a quick "thank you" sign. The combination of salt, crunch, and sweet was surprisingly tasty.

"I think I'm going to make these at home sometime," Peter said to Jake. "Now, where should we work today?"

Jake's sticky fingers picked up his talker, adeptly turned it on, and found the page he needed to be on. Jake punched in his response to Peter's question with ease. "Want out," he said. The device spoke Jake's request.

Peter looked outside and saw a beautiful patio with a view of Bridget's lush green lawn. "Out there?" Peter replied, pointing to the patio. Jake nodded yes, went back to his home screen, and punched "today." The device spoke his message again.

"Hmmm...today? Was today good, Jake? Did you make any new friends?" Peter asked. Jake nodded again and smiled broadly. "That's awesome, bud."

Jake turned back to the device to continue the conversation once more, and his fingers found the words, "Peter...today." Jake pointed to Peter as the device relayed his message.

"My day was excellent, Jake. I think it's going to be an awesome year for the both of us," Peter responded.

After they cleaned up the mess from Jake's snack, they headed outside on the patio, armed with the iPad, Jake's wireless speaker, and Peter's guitar. As was his routine, Jake played some of his favorite songs straight through the speaker and performed all of the movements. As always, Peter sang along and danced to the music. He didn't even have to fake the energy he needed for these sessions; Jake's mood was always contagious.

When the usual mix of songs was done, Jake grabbed his talker. He selected the symbols and the device spoke, "Dudes...song...new."

Even after so many years of hanging out with Jake, Peter was still amazed at the combination of simplicity and complexity that made him who he was. He was also impressed at how much Jake could communicate without ever uttering a single word.

"Gotcha," said Peter, picking up his phone. He did a quick search to figure out what their new song was called. These guys pumped out new songs like most people drank water, so Peter had to work hard to stay up to date. Luckily, their songs were aimed at the two-to-five-year-old audience, so Peter could learn the lyrics easily and pick up the tune by ear after a few listens and some trial and error. The new song had been released the previous week and was called "Beautiful Me." Peter took a moment to add it to Jake's iPad.

"Let's give it a listen, Jake, and you can tell me what you think," he said.

Jake sat at the picnic table. It was rare to see Jake sitting quietly without some part of him moving unless he was asleep or watching one of his favorite movies on the tablet. He looked as though he was ready to listen, so Peter synced his phone to Jake's speaker and pressed play. The song was slower than most of the Dudes' songs and a little more serious too. It sounded like a lullaby, and Jake was mesmerized and completely still from the first note.

Beautiful Me

When I wake up in the morning
And my hair is in my face
Still you see, still you see
Beautiful me

When you take my hand and lead me
Through the moments of my day
Still you see, still you see
Beautiful me

You love me and protect me
You encourage me to try
You sing to me and hold me
In the middle of the night
You smile when I am angry
You forgive me when I'm wrong

36

You find the good in bad things
You make me feel like I belong

Because you see, because you see
Beautiful me

When I forget to listen and
To everything you say
Still you see, still you see
Beautiful me

When your day is very busy
And you still find time to play
Still you see, still you see
Beautiful me

You love me and protect me
You encourage me to try
You sing to me and hold me
In the middle of the night
You smile when I am angry
You forgive me when I'm wrong
You find the good in bad things
You make me feel like I belong

Because you see, because you see
Beautiful me

When the world is so confusing
And you help me find my way
I know you see, you always see
Beautiful me

When you tell me I am special
At the end of every day
I know you see, you always see
Beautiful me

I know you see, you always see beautiful me

When the music stopped, all Peter could hear was the sound of the birds in the trees. Jake was so silent that Peter was concerned that he might be getting sick or something. He quietly stood up, walked over to where Peter's guitar rested against the seat of the picnic table, lifted it up, and placed it into Peter's hands. He sat back down in his chair and looked at Peter expectantly.

"Damn, Jake," chuckled Peter, "you give me way more credit than I deserve." Jake's intention was crystal clear: he wanted Peter to play the song, but having only just heard it for the first time, Peter wasn't so sure he would be able to. "What do you say we listen to it again a couple of times so I can learn it?" said Peter.

Jake nodded his head emphatically, said, "Ya...ya...ya," and he jumped up and down in circles, indicating his approval of the plan before settling in next to Peter to get to work.

That's how Emily found them when she returned from her run: the two boys were sitting head to head, leaned over Peter's guitar as he played. She watched for a moment as Peter fumbled slightly over the chords to a song she had never heard before. They were obviously tackling something new, and it was pretty clear that Jake was excited about it. She swore she could hear him singing, "Boooooo me," over and over again. Emily couldn't help but let a warm smile creep over her lips as she watched the pair. She had to admit that, together, they were definitely something special.

Chapter 5

Jake's Nighttime Dream Show

Emily let the warm water cascade over her body and wash the sweat and the stress of the day away. Today had warranted a long run, and she'd ended up going a little farther than her intended ten miles when she managed to get a little lost. No matter, though, because without planning it or knowing it, she had walked back in at the perfect time.

As she dried off and dressed back in her plaid skirt, Emily couldn't get the image of Jake and Peter out of her head. She had known Peter for so long that he was almost a fixture in her life. He was like an old workhorse, strong and reliable, and though he had been coming two to three times a week to hang out with Jake, Emily had never really noticed Peter. Until today. The bond that he and Jake shared was so incredible that she was almost a little bit jealous. But something had changed about him. When she had met Peter at the door today, she had noticed an unmistakable difference. His face had matured, and his large green eyes seemed brighter.

"Emily!" called her mom, breaking her free from her thoughts. "Are you almost ready to go? Aunt Bridget is here, and I want to get back in time to put Jake to bed."

"Two minutes, Mom!" she replied. "I'll be right there!"

Emily did not want to hesitate a second longer than necessary to go shopping. Mom had texted her earlier that day to say that a partial insurance check had been issued that they could use to buy some clothes. Dad had also just returned from his business trip and had contributed a little bit of money for essentials. Emily was walking on air thinking of shopping for clothes that fit and running shoes that weren't purchased at Walmart. Tomorrow was a new day, and a new day in some new, kick-ass clothes was exactly what Emily needed.

As they drove to the mall, Susan peppered Emily with the usual first-day-of-school-after-your-house-just-burnt-down series of questions. Emily answered them as best she could, relaying everything from how Jake had entered school to the reactions of his classmates to the embarrassment of having to sing the hug song. Susan smiled knowingly. "I've been there before," she said with a sigh. "I'm really sorry that you had to bring him to school today. Now that a little money is coming in, I'll try to take a little of the responsibility off of your plate, honey. If you can keep bringing him to school, I'll arrange to

41

work from seven to two so I can get him home. That will start next week. I can also call the school to see about having his teacher meet him at the entrance so you don't have to be burdened with walking him to resource."

Maybe it was the euphoria of impending shopping that came over her, but what Emily said next surprised even herself.

"You know what, Mom, don't bother calling the school. If it helps you out, I don't mind walking him all the way in in the morning."

"I'm so proud of you, baby," Susan replied.

The pair spent the next two hours giving Mom's credit card a pretty heavy workout. The went to Emily's favorite store, Lex's, for school and hang-out clothes, sweats, pajamas, and six pairs of heavenly fitting jeans in every style and wash available. Mom even bought a few things, which made Emily happy because she was getting sick of seeing her in the same army-green scrubs and Crocs every day for the past two weeks.

The next stop was the running store. Emily and Susan had been frequent customers here ever since Emily had taken a serious interest in running about six years before, and the owner knew Emily and Susan by name. He also knew Emily by size.

"I was hoping to see you two," he said. "I even set aside some shoes for you to try, Emily."

Emily smiled gratefully. He actually had a pretty good handle on what she liked and was well aware of the quality of shoe she needed to get her through the season. As usual, he was right on, and she chose two of the pairs he had set aside along with an entire new running wardrobe for training.

"These are on the house," he said, setting the most expensive pair of running sneakers aside. "I was really sorry to hear about your house."

Susan halfheartedly argued with the shop owner, knowing all too well how expensive Emily's specialty shoes were and how difficult it is to keep your head above water as a small business owner. In the end, he insisted, and Emily and Susan graciously thanked him.

"Run like the wind this season, Emily. That's the only thanks I need," he said as they left.

Emily intended, as always, to do exactly that.

Emily and Susan returned home to find Jake and Aunt Bridget spread out on the living room floor playing a game of Candy Land. Both of the dogs' heads were resting on Jake's lap as they slept peacefully, seemingly unaware of the level of competitiveness that Jake could create during a simple board game. Everyone knew that if anyone besides Jake drew the Queen Frostine card, all hell was going to break loose. Susan suspected that Bridget may have removed that one from the pile to avoid any unpleasantness before bedtime.

As soon as he saw them, Jake stood up and enveloped them both in a clumsy, slightly desperate, and off-balance hug. He pulled them close and clung to them as if they had been gone for years rather than just a few hours. Emily couldn't wait for him to release her so she could go upstairs and try on her new clothes. She broke free as soon as she possibly could and bolted toward the stairs with a quick, "Night, everyone! Thanks, Mom."

She had made it only halfway to the top when she heard Jake's slow, thick voice say, "Dah…Mimimimi, dah." This was Jake's way of telling her to stop.

Frustrated, she turned around to face her brother. "What, Jake?"

Jake responding by saying, "Mimi," as he did the sign for "bed." He looked at her expectantly, his tired eyes wordlessly pleading with her. She saw her mom in the background with the proud smile on her face that she always got when she sensed her two children were bonding. But Emily was not in the mood to give any further today. Jake was her brother, not her child, and she wanted to figure out what she was going to wear tomorrow, *not* put her fifteen-year-old perpetually toddler-like brother to bed.

"Not tonight, Jake," Emily replied abruptly as she turned back around and completed her ascent up the stairs and to her room. Although she never looked back, she could clearly feel the energy of pure disappointment radiating from both Jake and her mom. At that particular moment, she didn't really care. She closed the door firmly and purposefully and inhaled the sweet silence of her empty room.

Fifteen minutes later, with some help from Snapchat and Nat, she had the perfect outfit picked out for school. Emily was anticipating a much improved second day of her senior year, when compared to the first. As she started getting ready for bed, he could hear the muffled sound of giggling as Jake and her mother sang a duet of "Jake's Nighttime Dream Show." Her feeling of content anticipation mixed with a hint of guilt as she drifted off to sleep.

Chapter 6

Surprise

The next two weeks passed by quickly as Emily, Jake, and Susan got adjusted to their new routine. Cross-country training had started in earnest, and Emily was intently focused on her need for a spectacular season. As promised, she continued to drive Jake to school in the morning, while Susan picked him up and attended to his needs after school.

Emily walked him faithfully to his classroom each morning. Day by day, she noticed a change in the way his peers reacted to him as he entered the building. The change was not in Jake; he was as consistent as they come. Each day, he continued to stop random people, he continued to smile and greet them with his jovial babble, and he continued to model his cherished shirts. It was as if, from the beginning, he knew that he could be exactly who he was and that people would come around to understanding and accepting him in their own time.

That was precisely what happened. Within the first few days of school, kids had already stopped looking at him strangely. Initially, they began to patronize Jake with a quick high five or fist bump and an obligatory compliment about his shirt. But in the weeks that followed, Emily noticed that the kids were not only *responding* to Jake, they were *looking* for him. They were initiating interactions and anticipating Jake's arrival as a welcome part of their morning routine. Before long, a small group of freshmen and sophomores were waiting for Jake at the door to the side entrance each morning. They always greeted Emily politely, but they showered Jake with smiles, high fives, and spontaneous comments about whatever he chose to wear that day. Many from the group would bring Jake all the way to room 64. Sometimes, Emily felt invisible, but despite the fact that Jake commanded all of the attention, most days she felt a growing pride that Jake was her little brother.

There was one person that was not so easily won over, not by the positive energy that surrounded her brother and definitely not by his daily personal greetings. That person was Julie Wallace.

Ever since the day in the counselor's office, when Mr. Grant had revealed Gray Hat's identity, Emily had been trying to find a way to connect with her. For several days that first week, she said hello to Julie and reintroduced herself, but these attempts were met with silence. Every morning, Julie continued to sit in the same corner by the entrance to room 64. Every day, Jake tapped her on her covered head as she made herself as small as humanly possible. She lowered her head and scribbled intently, seemingly oblivious to the fact that dozens of other people shared that hallway with her. Emily had a feeling that Julie desperately wanted them all to disappear. This Julie was so far removed from the outgoing, always-smiling Julie she remembered from first grade. Emily sadly wondered what had happened to change her old friend into such an unrecognizable shell of her former self.

This wasn't to say that Jake hadn't made at least a little headway. By the beginning of the third week of school, instead of telling him to "get lost" or "buzz off," Julie simply ignored him and kept scribbling. Rather than snorting at their ritual "hug" song, she was kind enough to stay silent and let them carry on without comment. Today, even though Julie never lifted her head from her paper, Emily could swear she saw the slightest nod of Julie's head when Jake tapped her. Two things were certain when it came to Jake: First, he was as persistent as they come, and Emily was sure he would not give up until Julie became his best friend. Second, he had an uncanny sixth sense for those who were in need. Emily always thought this was sort of ironic considering how people always said that Jake was the one with "special needs." Coupled together, these things she knew about her brother intrigued Emily, and because of them, she was anxiously anticipating what the next couple of weeks might bring.

Nothing could have prepared Emily for what happened at the end of the third week of school. On Friday morning, Jake was greeted by his usual parade of admirers. He was wearing a bright red T-shirt with an Elmo face on it and black lettering that said "Elmo Loves YOU!". If Emily had to guess, this one was his absolute favorite. Jake's face was beaming brightly this morning as he listened to his classmates and admirers showering him with compliments. Emily was becoming more and more content trailing the crowd, being a silent observer and letting the comfort of this daily ritual warm her heart. Jake half walked, half skipped to the door of room 64, where his entourage said good-bye and headed off to their first period classes.

As she and Jake rounded the corner to his room, both stopped abruptly, their mouths open in shock as they looked quizzically at one another and then back to the corner, where Julie Wallace sat scrunched up as usual with a pad of paper on her lap. But today, she was looking up, and Emily noted an almost smile in her sad-but-beautiful gray-blue eyes. It was the first time either of them had truly seen her face. Jake seemed momentarily taken aback by this small change in routine, but after a brief moment of silence, Jake stretched out his Elmo shirt, said, "Ama!" and looked pointedly at Julie.

Julie gave him a brief thumbs-up and said, "Cool." What she did next, however, changed Emily's relationship with her forever.

Julie got to her feet as Emily watched her face cautiously for any indication of what might be happening. She was ready to jump in if there was even the slightest threat to Jake, whether physical or verbal. But Julie simply reached up and grabbed the top zipper of her black hoodie and pulled it down, revealing the bright blue Cookie Monster shirt that she wore underneath. She pulled the sides of her sweatshirt apart and faced Jake directly, her smile brightening with each passing second. She looked at Emily only briefly before casting her eyes down toward the floor, as if her plan stopped here and she had no idea what to do next. Jake took care of that by jumping up and down, putting his hands up in a "victory" gesture before turning to Emily to request the hug song. It was as if he knew that this breakthrough was enough for today. Emily let the air out of her lungs in a long sigh, having not realized how long she had been holding her breath or how anxious she had been feeling. "Thank you, Julie," she whispered as Julie sank back down into her usual position in the corner. Julie's cheeks were pink from the experience, but her eyes looked as if they held a little more life inside of them. She zipped up her hoodie and focused her attention back on her pad. "My pleasure," she mumbled.

Emily and Jake sang their daily duet and went their separate ways. Emily felt strangely happy all day long.

Chapter 7

Peanut Butter Crackers

Emily spent an obscene amount of time in the shower when she arrived home on Friday afternoon. Cross-country practice had been especially grueling in the unseasonable late-September heat, so she let her thoughts and worries drift away with the steam and focused only on the moment. One thing was for certain about Aunt Bridget: she had extremely good taste in decorating. At their old house, Emily had shared a bathroom with Jake and her mom. At Aunt Bridget's house, she had a bathroom to herself. Not only a bathroom but a glorious one, complete with multiple shower heads at every position and angle and beautiful earth-toned tile that made her feel like she was at a resort.

Only when she felt as though she had washed away every sticky inch of sweat from her body did Emily finally step out of the shower. Thankfully, even though her legs were still weak from conditioning, she felt energized and excited. Tonight was going to be epic...or at least she hoped it would be. She would be hanging out with Warren. How could that not be incredible?

The six of them—Emily, Nat, Sophie, Robert, EJ, and Warren—had made plans at the lunch table today. They decided they would all get together at Robert's house tonight. They had talked about doing all of the usual things, like dinner, movies, or bowling, but in the end, the heat had dictated that Robert's house might be a better choice. *Humph*, thought Emily. *House—that's an understatement.*

Mansion or mini-resort might have been a better way to describe where Robert lived. Emily hadn't actually been there in years, not since his tenth birthday party, but she remembered it well. His house had a giant pool complete with two slides, a stone waterfall, a hot tub for at least twenty-five people, and a game room that put Chuck E. Cheese to shame. The Boon family was definitely not hurting for money.

The butterflies crept up, one by one, as she got dressed and dried and straightened her hair. By the time she was ready to go, they were thundering uncontrollably inside of her. She glanced at her phone, which read 7:25. Luckily, there was plenty of time before she had to leave, but right now, the quiet of her room was amplifying her feelings of anxiety. She went downstairs to see what was going on.

The silence that greeted her at the bottom of the stairs was a surprise. Aunt Bridget was away for the weekend, and her mom had to work late, but Emily was certain that Jake and Peter were home. For someone that was considered nonverbal, Jake managed to be pretty loud, especially when Peter was around. Emily stopped to listen for the boys and eventually heard the sound of rustling paper coming from the living room. She walked quietly toward the sound and peeked through the doorway. The boys were so engrossed in what they were doing that they didn't notice her for a good three minutes. Again, she was mesmerized by the interaction between Jake and Peter. It was almost as though Peter could read Jake's mind—a superpower that Emily herself wished that she possessed on a daily basis. Feelings of envy weaved their way between the butterflies, leaving Emily feeling a bit confused. For sure, Peter understood her brother, and all his wonderful complexities, far better than she did.

Peter looked up at her as Jake continued his full-on concentration on coloring. Jake's tongue was out as he gripped the orange crayon in his fist. Peter, for his part, held the paper in place so it wouldn't be destroyed under the force of Jake's hands. The scene was so unlike their usual routine that Emily shot a questioning look at Peter as she considered what on earth could possibly be motivating her brother to do the thing he hated most in the world: coloring. Peter met her eyes and smiled knowingly. "This," he said triumphantly, his green eyes shining with pride, "is a very special project and a little bit of a mystery. Jake says that we should warn you, though, it's top secret."

Then he turned to Jake with a quick wink and asked, "What do you think, bud, should we let her in on it?"

It was at that point that Jake finally noticed her standing there. His gigantic grin melted her heart as he nodded his head emphatically and patted his hand on the floor beside him. She immediately sat down beside him and draped her arm over his broad shoulders.

"I think that's a yes!" Peter said, chuckling. "Do you want to tell her or should I?"

"Ma," Jake replied pointing to himself. He grabbed his talker and pushed repeat, making the device repeat the last thing Jake had tried to communicate. Emily listened carefully to the resulting message. "Card...roar...running...hat...room 64."

Jake looked at her expectantly as Peter turned to her and whispered, "That's the mystery part. I know what we're doing, but I don't know *who* we're doing it for. I assume there's a 'young lady' involved. What else would motivate Jake to...dare I even say it...to *color*?" Peter faked a gag as he spoke.

Suddenly, his expression changed, and Emily noticed his gaze drift ever-so-quickly down the length of her white sundress and back up to her face again. "Oh, I'm sorry, Emily. You were probably headed out. Go ahead, I'll figure this out."

Emily put her hand briefly on his back. "No worries," she said, glancing at the clock. "I've got some time *and*…I think I can help solve your mystery." Peter raised his eyebrows questioningly, and she briefly relayed the story of the past few weeks, including their morning routine and the story of Jake's breakthrough with the girl in the corner this morning. "Hat…64. I think it means the girl in the gray hat that sits outside of Jake's classroom in the morning." She turned to Jake. "Jake, do you want to invite Julie to RAWWR next Saturday?" she asked.

"Ma ma, ya," Jake responded, jumping up and down before he enveloped both Emily and Peter in a giant hug. RAWWR stood for Regional Annual Walk Wheel Run, an annual fundraiser for special needs programs and grants in the area. Susan was very involved in the organization.

Even though she was feeling slightly claustrophobic, Emily couldn't help but smile into the soft warmth of Jake's Big Bird T-shirt. Maybe she was a mind reader after all. Or maybe she just knew a little bit more about her brother than she gave herself credit for.

When Jake finally released them, Peter gently held Jake's face, in order to make sure he was listening, and teased him. "Oh?? Do you have a girlfriend? I *knew* it!"

Jake's pink cheeks translated that he completely understood what Peter was implying. He smiled shyly and shook his head, saying, "Na na na na!"

"Actually," Emily clarified, "the girl in the gray hat is Julie Wallace. Remember her, from like first and second grade? I used to be really good friends with her. She would come over all the time to play. The three of us used to spend hours climbing trees in the woods between our houses. I remember your mom bringing us lemonade and cookies."

"Are you serious? Of course I remember her!" Peter said. "I heard that she was back at school. I even saw a few pictures of her on Instagram over the summer, but that girl looks nothing like Julie."

"I know, right?" Emily said. "The only reason I know it's her is because, on the first day of school, I was called to Mr. Grant's office because he wanted to check in with me after the fire. When I left, she was waiting to see him. He called her by name. I keep trying to see a small resemblance to the girl we used to know, but I can't find it. She just looks so sad. I've tried to talk to her when I drop Jake off in the morning, but she doesn't even acknowledge that I'm there."

They talked for a few more minutes about their memories of Julie from when they were young. Both of them agreed that what they remembered most vividly was her carefree spirit and huge smile. They speculated for a moment or two about the reason for the dramatic change, before turning their attention back to Jake.

"Apparently coloring is exhausting," Emily said to Peter.

Jake was still sitting on the floor, but he was now slumped, almost motionless, against the base of the oversized beige linen couch. He looked like a giant baby panda bear about to roll into the hay for a nap.

"Let's get you ready for bed, bud," Peter said, grabbing his left arm gently and attempting to coax him to a standing position. "We'll let your sister head out to wherever the popular folks are gathering tonight."

Surprisingly, Jake jumped up suddenly. He broke free of Peter's grasp and grabbed Emily's hand. "Ka ka," he said. "Mimi." He pointed to the staircase as he spoke

"What, Jake?" she asked.

He grabbed his talker, adeptly found the "food" page, and hit "cracker." Emily froze as she took a moment to process what he was trying to say. It had been many years since he had asked her to sing that song. It had always been one of her favorites. She would sing it to him when he was younger while helping Mom give him a bath. Back then, he seemed like a toy to her. He had once been her absolute favorite plaything and her own personal living baby doll. It seemed like a lifetime ago, but she had once adored helping Mom take care of him.

"Crap," she muttered under her breath as she saw the time displayed at the top of the talker screen. It was 8:30. She had planned on leaving at 8:00 for Robert's house.

"Sure, Jake," she said more brightly than she felt. "Let's get ready for bed. You're way too old for me to give you a bath, but Peter and I can hang with you, and you can show us how you wash up and get ready for bed. OK?"

"Yayaya," was Jake's only response, but he nodded and practically sprinted up the stairs.

Then, she looked at Peter. "Are you familiar with the 'Peanut Butter Cracker' song?" she said with a smile, trying desperately to conceal how conflicted she was suddenly feeling.

"Hmmm…I don't believe I am," Peter said with a hint of surprise in his voice. When it came to music, even kid's music, Peter knew almost everything.

"Well then, you are in for a treat. This is a Prescott family original, and Jake and I are going to teach *you* a song for once," Emily teased.

Emily and Peter walked side by side to Jake's bathroom at the top of the staircase. Emily could already hear the water running as they reached the landing. When they walked, single file, through the door, Emily saw that Jake had already picked up his toothbrush. She and Peter perched on the edge of the giant spa bathtub for a moment while Jake consulted the visual schedule that Mom had hung on the bathroom mirror. It outlined, in pictures, each small step Jake needed to complete before bed. No matter how many times Jake had completed this routine, he could not remember every part of it. Years ago, Mom had learned to post a sequence of pictures to help him get things done more independently and with less prompting from the family. It worked like a charm, and now they were posted almost everywhere and for any routine you could imagine.

Jake turned to Emily and motioned for her to stand up. "Mmm, mmm, GA!" he said with an intonation so specific Emily knew that, while his mouth was not quite forming the words, his mind was saying, "Ready…set…go." It was time for her to sing.

Together, Jake and Emily peered into the mirror and smiled. Emily looked behind her at Peter's reflection and said, "Feel free to join in on round two. The more the merrier."

Jake consulted his visual schedule and went about completing the tasks as he simultaneously danced along to Emily's singing. Emily was secretly impressed at how independent he had become.

Peanut butter cracker
Peanut butter cracker
Peanut butter cracker in my hair hair hair
Wash it wash it wash it
Scrub it scrub it scrub
Get that silly cracker out of there there there

Peanut butter cracker
Peanut butter cracker
Peanut butter cracker in my ear ear ear
Wash it wash it wash it
Scrub it scrub it scrub it
Get that silly cracker out of here here here

Peanut butter cracker
Peanut butter cracker
Peanut butter cracker on my face face face
Wash it wash it wash it
Scrub it scrub it scrub it
Keep that silly cracker in its place place place

Peanut butter cracker
Peanut butter cracker
Peanut butter cracker on my feet feet feet
Wash it wash it wash it
Scrub it scrub it scrub it

Save that silly cracker just to eat eat eat

Peanut butter cracker
Peanut butter cracker
Peanut butter cracker in my mouth mouth mouth
Wash it wash it wash it
Scrub it scrub it scrub it
Get those silly cracker crumbs all out out out

As expected, Peter quickly learned the words and the rhythm of the song. He wholeheartedly belted it out until Jake had finished all the tasks and was ready for bed.

"Nice job, Prescott family. That one is a classic!" he chuckled. "Thank you. But now, I insist that you get out of here, I am all set to get this guy to bed."

"I am totally taking you up on that! I am beyond late, but for Jake, Warren can wait," Emily said hurriedly.

Emily swore she saw a brief frown cross Peter's face, and the thought nagged at her as she got into the Jeep and finally headed off to Robert's house. Before she started the car, she sent a text to the group, letting them know she would be there in fifteen minutes.

Maybe Warren could wait, but Emily didn't think she could hold on much longer before seeing him.

Chapter 8

Stand Up and Move

Emily was still flying high when Monday morning came. Though she had been incredibly late getting to Robert's on Friday, the night had been well worth the wait. Her friends had been hanging out by the pool when she arrived. Four of them were roasting marshmallows around the fire pit, and Warren appeared to be dozing off on top of an adorable frog-shaped floatie in the pool. Emily was happy to see that his eyes were closed, and she took full advantage of that fact by sneaking a subtle peek at his abs, which were pretty impressive. Emily pulled the bottom of her sundress up and sat at the edge of the pool, dipping her feet in the cool, clear water. She hadn't thought to buy a new swimsuit after the fire so she didn't plan on going in. Warren opened his eyes and swam over to her as soon as she sat down. He rested his chin between his hands, his elbows turned outward on either side of him on the edge of the pool. He turned his head toward her, resting his cheek on the stonework, as they chatted. Over time, he inched himself closer and closer to her, until he was eventually close enough to touch her. He placed his damp hands on her hips and pulled her in to the shallow water along with him, holding her loosely against him as they continued their first, somewhat intimate conversation. If any of the others had noticed them, Emily was unaware because, at that moment, nobody else existed in the world. He kissed her three times before they emerged, hand in hand, from the water and took their place in a lounge chair by the fire with their friends. She had dried off sitting on his lap by the fire and could still recall vividly the feeling of the damp dress pressed against her legs and the warmth of pure bliss in her soul.

That feeling carried her through the rest of the weekend, so much so that she was actually looking forward to school on Monday morning. She was ready fifteen minutes earlier than usual, which gave her plenty of time to help Jake finish getting his breakfast ready. They packed up his books and lunch, grabbed his iPad, and headed out the door five minutes ahead of schedule. That would be five fewer minutes before she could see Warren.

But about ten minutes into their ride to school, Jake began frantically emptying his backpack onto the floor of the Jeep. He took each book, pen, pencil, folder, and stray piece of paper out of every pocket. "What's going on, Jake?" Emily asked, feeling a little surprised at the look of pure panic on Jake's face.

Jake responded by saying, "Uh...uh...uh." But Emily could feel stress in the air just as plainly as she could see the stricken look on his face. When he was anxious, the words had an even more difficult time finding their way out of his mouth. Finally, he pulled out his iPad and said, "Card...hat...run."

Emily let out a few choice words under her breath. She knew they would have to turn around and go back home. Jake's stubborn streak was a mile wide; she had learned that from experience. She doubted she would be able to get him out of the car and into school without the invitation for Julie.

Damnit! she thought. *So much for being early for once.* Now, she would have to wait until lunch to catch up with Warren.

She pulled off into the drugstore parking lot and turned around to go back to Aunt Bridget's.

Ultimately, they made it through the front door of the school exactly ninety seconds before the first period bell rang. The halls were almost empty, which meant that Jake's fan club was not present to greet them today. If Emily was being honest, that was a little disappointing, but Jake was focused on a bigger mission. He didn't even seem to notice that it was just the two of them walking down the echoing hallway.

Luckily, Julie didn't seem to be in much of a hurry to get to her first period class. She was crouched in the corner, still looking very comfortable, when they arrived at the entrance to room 64. Today her long, wavy-blond hair fell freely over her shoulders and across her face as she looked down at her sketch pad. There was no gray hat in sight. She looked up and smiled when she sensed Jake standing above her.

"Good morning, Jake," she said quietly and managed a shy, "Hi," in Emily's direction. "I didn't think I was going to see you this morning."

"Ha," Jake managed with a flamboyant wave and a slight bow that rustled the paper he was holding in his hand. Emily rolled her eyes a bit at his behavior. He was always so over the top. It did make her chuckle, though. She just wished he would get on with it so she could actually get to class. But, of course, the next thing he did was request her assistance with a song by saying, "Moo," as he signed "stand" in her direction.

Crap, was all Emily could think. The morning had started off heavenly but had quickly become a roller coaster. There was no time to waste; Jake wanted to ask Julie to stand up and, yes, there was a song for that.

Emily cleared her throat and started singing "Stand Up and Move" to the best of her ability. Jake signed along and joined in where he could, which mostly included his approximations of up, move, and dance.

> *Stand up and MOVE (move move)*
> *Stand up and MOVE (move move)*
> *Stand up and MOVE right up onto your feet*

> *Stand up and DANCE (dance dance)*
> *Stand up and DANCE (dance dance)*
> *Stand up and dance (dance dance) to the beat*

Mercifully, Julie understood almost immediately what Jake was requesting. She brushed her hair from her face, put her pad on the floor next to where she was sitting, and stood up. She looked Jake calmly in the eye and said, "What's up?"

With great gusto, Jake presented the invitation. Julie held it in her hands, admiring it while complimenting Jake on his artwork. She appeared to be genuinely touched and impressed. After a moment or two, she turned and looked quizzically at Emily. A quick glance at the colorful paper made Emily realize that there were no actual words on the invitation. Thinking quickly, Jake picked up his talker and attempted to clarify. "Card…64…running…RAWWR," he said, and looked expectantly at a slightly confused Julie. By then, Mrs.

Lawrence, Jake's teacher, had opened the door and was looking for him. She waited patiently to see how this played out.

Emily jumped in to explain. "Jake has a special needs walk/run event, called 'RAWWR,' at Sawyer Park on Saturday. He wanted to invite you to come. It starts at ten, but it's a huge fundraiser so you have to get there pretty early to find parking. He would really like you to be there."

"Okay," Julie managed. "Thank you, Jake," she said sincerely, smiling brightly. "I would love to come."

Emily quickly interrupted the moment. She was getting pretty stressed about being late to class. "Julie," she said, "would you mind giving me your cell number? I can text you the details and confirm that you can be there later today. Right now, I'm late for first period, and I really hate being late."

Emily tried to hide her frustration at Julie's hesitation. Finally, Julie agreed, and the two exchanged numbers. "Thanks!" Emily called over her shoulder as she hurried away. "I'll get you the information later today."

Not two seconds later, Emily heard a voice from behind her. "Excuse me, Miss! Where is your hall pass?" It was Mr. Sylvester, the assistant principal and glorified hall monitor. When she turned to respond, he realized who she was. "Ah, good morning, Emily. Let me walk you to class," he offered.

That was one perk to having a sibling with special needs: people usually assumed you had a good reason for breaking the rules.

Chapter 9

Eat

Julie sat in the corner seat of the farthest table she could find from the "popular" kids. Being the new kid in school was not foreign to her. She and her mom had moved at least four times since she first left Brighton, and now they were back for her senior year of high school. Normally, it was her goal to swallow her pride and do what she had to do to make friends immediately. In the past, that had been a cakewalk because she had been blessed with an outgoing personality and very little fear. She had not anticipated how the events of the summer would make this transition unlike any other.

After more than three weeks, Julie had to admit that she was getting kind of tired of eating lunch by herself. In fact, she was getting tired of doing everything by herself, but by now she had earned herself the reputation of being a hermit, at the very least. Her only consolation was that the other reputation she had recently inherited was far worse, and it was only partially her fault. The other guilty parties were walking around completely unscathed.

"Mama!"

The now-familiar combination of that utterance and a shadow standing above her woke her from her pity party. She was somewhat surprised to see Jake, along with his helper, Mrs. Anderson, zeroing in on her once again today. "Oh," she said with a slight smile, "hey, Jake." Julie was accustomed to Jake's presence in the morning, but his appearance at lunch today was new and unnerving.

Jake held his palm flat out toward Julie in a clear "wait" signal and shuffled off toward the other side of the cafeteria. Mrs. Anderson was hot on his heels. Julie's curiosity was piqued as her gaze followed him across the room. It was probably the first time she had ever looked up for this long during lunch, and it definitely felt foreign. It was as if she'd stepped out into the sunlight for the first time after spending a month in a darkened room.

Her stomach clenched tightly as Jake approached Robert at the end of the popular table, and she had to look away before anyone made eye contact with her. It was still too raw and painful.

She turned her head to the side, using her peripheral vision to keep an eye on things. She saw Jake tap Emily on the shoulder. Emily looked at him, momentarily confused at the unanticipated interruption. Julie saw Jake jump up and down slightly, as he did when he was excited, and make what looked like a gesture or sign, his fingers pointed toward his lips. Julie was relieved that Jake seemed focused only on Emily. *This might not end too badly*, Julie thought. Emily seemed unaware of anything that had happened between her friends and Julie. It was probably why she was the only one of them to acknowledge that Julie existed.

Emily arose, somewhat slowly, from her chair and followed Jake. She appeared reluctant and unhappy. Jake returned to the table and stood over Julie again. Emily followed behind at a short distance. Julie's heart raced, and she was thankful that Jake had chosen to stand in front of her, blocking the popular table's view of her face.

"Mama," repeated Jake. He turned to Emily and made the same gesture he had made when he approached her lunch table. She looked at Julie and gently explained, "Jake is signing 'eat,' and he wants to ask you something." In the safety of Jake's shadow, Julie ventured a glance at Emily. Her face was flushed and pink with embarrassment, and it made the knot in Julie's stomach clench tighter, especially because Emily always seemed cool and calm.

"As you probably guessed," Emily mumbled softly, "he needs my help to ask you something, so let's get this over with as quickly as possible."

Jake signed "eat" again. It felt as if every eye in the cafeteria was on them. Julie thanked God silently for the simple shade of Jake's shadow.

Emily turned to Jake and said, "You can start this song, Jake, you know this one."

Jake nodded his head emphatically and began singing "EEEEEEE, EEEEEE." Just as Emily started quietly and cautiously singing the next words, Peter came up behind her, placed his hand softly on her shoulder, and began singing right along with her. Julie could see Emily's body relax now that she was no longer singing solo in the middle of the cafeteria.

She could now be humiliated in good company.

Peter clapped briskly to the rhythm of the song and sang along with Jake:

> *Eat, eat, such a treat*
> *Come on friend, come take a seat*
>
> *Hey, hey look my way*
> *I want to eat with YOU today*

Peter and Emily repeated the song three times, Peter singing at the top of his lungs while Emily slouched over and mouthed the words, clearly praying for the song to be over.

Jake, for his part, filled in words where he could, pointing to Julie every time they sang the word "you."

When the singing stopped, it became awkwardly silent throughout the cafeteria for a moment. Peter turned to Julie. "Julie, I'm Peter, Peter McKinley. We used to hang out back in the day. Would you like to come eat lunch with me, my good friend Jake, and a bunch of drama geeks?" His green eyes sparkled as he looked at her. It made Julie smile too, despite her embarrassment.

Julie had regained her composure internally. *Well*, she thought, *that wasn't so bad*. It was like Jake had read her mind. She responded by looking at Jake and saying, "A girl would be a fool to turn down an invitation like that."

Peter grabbed Jake's hand while Jake held on to Julie's. Just like that, they snaked through the cafeteria to Jake's lunch table.

Julie ate lunch in the company of Peter, Jake, and a band of absolutely delightful drama geeks every day for the rest of her senior year.

Chapter 10

RAWWR

"Card hat run, card hat run." Jake constructed the message once, when he woke up on Saturday morning, and hit repeat on his device a thousand times. Every once in a while, he threw in a verbal "ROAARRRR," just for effect. Emily was expected to respond, each time, with reassurance that Julie would, in fact, be there to see Jake run. By 8:00 a.m., it was all Emily could do to refrain herself from seizing the damn talker and stomping it to pieces.

Jake's excitement was the only thing that kept her from carrying out her plan.

Emily had sent all of the specifics to Julie early in the week, as promised, and Julie had agreed to meet them at the park, under the registration tent at 9:20 a.m. Emily had confirmed the plan with Julie again last night. *"Gotcha, see you tomorrow!"* had been Julie's response at 9:28 p.m. Friday night.

The next morning, the Prescotts arrived at Sawyer Park at 8:30 a.m. sharp. The park was already abuzz with activity. There were kids of all ages, diagnoses, and abilities, running, walking, and wheeling around the beautiful park. There were already tons of kids playing on the large inclusive playground next to the track. It was one of the reasons that Sawyer Park was chosen for this regional event every year: the playground was designed to be accessible to all children, including those with special needs. Emily clearly remembered being at the dedication of the playground, maybe about five years ago. Since then, Jake had enjoyed playing here literally hundreds of times.

Susan was the chair of RAWWR, as she had been for the past several years. As soon as they had pulled into a parking space at Sawyer Park, she quickly rushed off to greet the masses of runners and volunteers and to delegate various jobs. By 8:45 a.m., Jake's coach arrived and gathered Jake's teammates to find a place to warm up.

Once Jake was off, Emily wandered around for a bit, taking a rare free moment to close her eyes and inhale the day. It was, honestly, a brilliant morning: one of those early fall days that held just the right combination of crisp air, warm sunshine, and cloudless cobalt sky.

Ten minutes later, her brief escape was interrupted.

"Emily! Emily! EMILY!" she heard in the distance. She opened her eyes, oriented herself and trotted off toward the sound of her mother's voice. "Could you place these posters on the wooden post beside the tent?"

- She handed Emily a roll of duct tape and three posters: one pink, one orange, and one green. The colors corresponded to the groups that the runners were in, and they would be used to display the schedule of start times and the results. She saw that Jake would be running in the first heat, which began at 10:15 a.m. Jake would be happy with that. He knew that once he was done running, he would be able to visit the snack shack. Jake loved a hard-earned burger.

As Emily worked, she kept a keen eye out for Julie's bright blue Honda. She didn't want Julie to feel overwhelmed by the growing crowd or have to navigate through it to find her. She also wanted to make sure that Julie got the best seat in the house to watch Jake run, primarily so he could see her rather than the other way around. Jake was actually a pretty graceful runner, and he had finished in the top three for the past five years. Last year, he had won. Julie knew that the best seat in the house would be at the finish line this year. Jake was surprisingly competitive when it came to this race, and his reaction to winning was always priceless. Emily wanted to see Julie's response almost as much as she wanted to see Jake's celebration.

It was almost 9:45 a.m. by the time she finished hanging the posters and directing various participants. She looked up from her work and scanned the crowd for Julie. When there was still no sign of her or of her car, Emily took out her phone to see if she had texted. No word from her either. "I knew I couldn't trust her," muttered Emily.

She shot her a final text: *"Heading over to the finish line. Jake is in the first heat, which starts at 10:15. Call me when you get here."*

Emily let out a sarcastic chuckle. *I should have said 'if' you get here*, she thought as she jogged toward the track. She was disheartened and bitter that Julie had not kept her promise to Jake. She tried her best to summon the joy she usually felt watching her brother shine at this event.

She checked her phone one more time, at 10:12 a.m., before making one more desperate scan of the crowds for some sign of Julie. There was none.

The announcer's voice came over the speaker, announcing the final call for the "Eagle" division, which encompassed the participants from fourteen to seventeen years of age. Emily could see Jake's back around the track in the distance. Even though she knew he couldn't hear her, she cheered loudly along with the hundreds of other supporters.

The loud popping of a large confetti cannon indicated the start of the race. Emily saw Jake, in his bright-green Oscar the Grouch shirt, start to move. As he rounded the first bend of the track, Emily saw that he and Frank Michaels were pulling away from the pack. As he came around the second bend, she saw that Jake had at least ten feet on Frank and at least twenty-five on the rest of the pack. As he rounded the third bend and entered the final straight, Emily could see the spectacular grin begin to light up his face. She was so focused on etching that look into her memory that she did not notice the commotion behind her.

As he entered fully into the final straight, Jake raised his head, searching for Susan and Emily just before his anticipated moment of triumph. When his eyes focused on them, he suddenly stopped midstride and dropped himself down in the middle of the track. His smiled faded quickly, and his eyes locked downward on his feet. He had actually been looking for Emily, Susan, *and* Julie. When he saw only two of them, disappointment crashed over him like a massive weight that was too much to bear.

Most of the participants were able to make their way around him to continue on toward the finish line. Some of the less-observant runners ran directly into him before they managed to regain their balance and complete the race. Without a word, Emily and Susan made their way toward the nearest entrance to the track, but it seemed to take forever in the crowd of tightly packed people watching the race. A loud *clank* of the chain link fence caught Emily's attention. She turned around and saw Julie jumping the height of the fence in one graceful movement. As soon as she landed, she ran wildly toward Jake, who continued to sit in the middle of the track. Some of the slower runners and walkers were still weaving around him.

Emily saw the look of confusion on Susan's face but quickly reassured her. "Don't worry, Mom, that's Julie," Emily said.

Emily and Susan were almost to the gate by the time Julie reached Jake. She crouched down on the track in front of him, holding something yellow in her hand and trying to coax him to stand up. Obviously, she had not yet been acquainted with his stubborn streak. Julie looked disheveled and stressed. As Emily moved closer to her, she could hear her saying, "I am so sorry, Jake," over and over again. As expected, Jake refused to look at anything besides his shoes—until Julie did something completely unexpected.

Julie stood up, looked directly at Jake, and started singing:

> *Stand up and move (move move)*
> *Stand up and move (move move)*
> *Stand up and move right up onto your feet*
>
> *Stand up and run (run run)*
> *Stand up and run (run run)*

Stand up and run to the finish line with me!

She sang it once, rather quietly, surprising Jake into making eye contact, which gave Julie the confidence to sing more loudly the second time. Sure enough, Jake got to his feet.

Julie took his hand and began to run in place until Jake started to move alongside her. They finished the race, crossing the finish line hand in hand and singing together at the top of their lungs. Jake's smile not only returned, but it magnified. He didn't care that he had finished dead last. He only cared that his friend was there.

Jake celebrated by wrapping Julie in an enormous embrace before walking away to show off the participation medal he had just been handed. As soon as he turned away, Julie bent over at the waist, placed her face in her hands, and began to cry.

Susan followed Jake as Emily approached Julie, touching her cautiously on the back. In response, Julie crumpled completely to the ground and began sobbing uncontrollably for a minute or two before lifting her face to look at Emily.

"I...am...so...sorry," she choked out. "I...I...I...never meant to hurt him."

Honestly, Emily was still pretty pissed off that Julie had broken her promise, but looking at her now made her heart break for Julie.

Julie wiped her nose on her long-sleeved yellow Big Bird shirt and continued, "Jake is my only friend. He's the only person who has acknowledged that I exist in this entire month of hell. He's the only person who's extended an invitation and made me feel included. I would never intentionally break a promise to him."

Emily looked at Julie, believing every word she said. Nonetheless, she was still confused and, feeling as though Julie might want to explain further, Emily simply said, "Well, then, why did you?"

Julie quickly and breathlessly went on to explain that her mom's car tire had been flat when she left for work at five in the morning. She had taken Julie's car instead and, not wanting to wake her, she had left a note on the kitchen table. The only problem was that Julie had left her phone in the glove compartment because, in her own words, "It's not like many people want to talk to me." When Julie woke up, she made her way downstairs, saw the note, and immediately started running. She ran the entire six miles from her house to the park.

"Wow, girl," Emily said out of pure sympathy and in order to brighten Julie's mood. "Maybe you should think about doing cross-country with me."

"Yeah," Julie replied as she half-laughed through her remaining tears, "and I only stopped once to grab these at the Quik Mart." Julie held out a yellow package of sour worms. They were Jake's favorite food in the entire world.

"You really speak his language," said Emily with a smile. "Maybe you should give those to him before he fills up on burgers and fries. But, before you head over there, I want you to know that I understand. This was absolutely beyond your control. I'm not gonna lie, I was really pissed when you weren't here at the start of the race. I totally thought you blew Jake off. What happened couldn't be helped and anyone who is willing to run six miles, hop a six-foot chain link fence, and publicly sing a 'Dudes' song for my brother deserves a second chance. The fact that you somehow know what his favorite snack is...well...that's also pretty impressive. I'll let you in on a small secret: Jake can be stubborn as hell, but he never holds a grudge if you come bearing food. That was a smart move, Julie."

Julie let out a long slow breath, cracked a real smile for the first time all day, and said, "I think I need a nap."

"I don't blame you one bit," Emily replied, "but before you doze off, let's go grab a burger and fries with Jake. My treat."

Chapter 11

Seeds of Doubt

The rest of the weekend was warm and rainy. On Sunday, Peter came over to hang out with Jake for a little while. Emily and her crew went to Robert's to hang out, play pool, and watch movies in his rec room. Warren had been there too, and he and Emily continued to hit it off really nicely.

Monday came, and the rain continued. The ground was so saturated that Emily's cross-country meet was cancelled before she even got to school. As soon as Emily found out, she texted Sophie and Nat, who played varsity soccer. They were supposed to play an away game in East Hurston, but their game was cancelled too. It was really rare for all three girls to have a day off from sports together. They quickly made plans to watch the boys' soccer game, which was scheduled to be at home, on the turf after school. Warren, Robert, and Sophie's boyfriend, EJ, were all on the team. Emily was looking forward to watching the game with her friends. She was also looking forward to having an excuse to stare at Warren for a solid hour without being considered a stalker.

As they entered the school that morning, she followed behind as Jake and his usual entourage squeaked down the hallway in wet sneakers. He was wearing his RAWWR T-shirt and participation medal this morning, which, predictably, was in the shape of a T. rex head. Jake showed it to everyone and got more handshakes and high fives than the President of the United States that morning. He was almost floating on air by the time they reached room 64, where Julie was sitting in her usual corner, looking bright eyed and well rested. "Hey, Julie!" Emily said. "How was the rest of your weekend?"

"Pretty quiet," Julie replied, "thank goodness. I had enough excitement on Saturday morning to last me for another week or two." She turned to Jake and said, "Good morning, buddy." In return, Jake wrapped her in an extra-exuberant hug. When he released her, he held up his medal, jumping up and down, and pointed to himself and to Julie. Julie giggled and said. "I know, Jake! I remember. You were amazing, and I had so much fun!" She then turned to Emily and said, "I'm so relieved that he only seems to remember the good stuff."

"Ba ba," Jake said as Mrs. Lawrence peeked out and called him to join her in room 64.

"Bye, Jake!" the girls said in unison.

86

When she was momentarily alone with Julie, Emily suddenly had an idea. She turned to Julie and said, "Hey! What are you doing after school?"

"Not much," Julie said with a smile that was showing itself more and more often lately. "Why do you ask?"

"Sophie, Nat, and I are going to watch the boys' soccer game. Want to come with?"

Julie visibly deflated before Emily's eyes. "Not today. I think I'm just going to head home after school. Thanks, though. Gotta go," she said flatly as she picked up her backpack and headed quickly down the hallway.

"Whoa, what just happened?" Emily muttered. She was standing, suddenly and awkwardly, alone at the entrance of room 64. With nothing else to do at the moment, she headed off to class, but all day she couldn't shake the strange feeling Julie had left her with.

The rain stopped around noon, and the sun came out. At the end of the day, Emily met Sophie and Nat in the atrium, and they ran across the street for a quick iced coffee before the game. The freedom to be a carefree teenager felt so welcome to all of them, even if it was for just a single afternoon.

Rather than sit on the bleachers, the girls stood against the fence to watch the game. Sophie wanted to be close to EJ, who played goalie for the team. The Brighton boys' team was ranked #2 and the East Hurston team was ranked #3, so the game promised to at least be a competitive one. A good game was obviously not the top priority for Emily; she had another motivation for being here.

Warren ran to the center forward position on the field at the start of the game. He scanned the bleachers briefly and then noticed the girls by the fence. He gave Emily a quick wink and grin before putting his game face on. Emily felt a warmth spread across her face, and she couldn't help but smile back.

The game was a very physical one from the beginning. EJ made three amazing saves in the first four minutes of the game to keep it scoreless. After a few defensive adjustments, it was all Brighton for the rest of the first half. Warren had three shots on goal, the final of which made its way into the net. As Emily watched the boys celebrate, she suddenly felt a presence beside her. She looked to her right and was surprised to see Peter casually leaning against the fence. "Good afternoon," he said.

"Hey, Peter," Emily said. "What are you doing here?"

"The better question," Peter said with a smile, "is what are *you* doing here? I try to come to all of the games so I can do the updates on Twitter. I don't think I've ever seen *you* here, though."

"The rain helped—no cross-country today for *once*," Emily responded.

"Gotcha," said Peter. "Can you do me a favor? I don't think we'll be staying much longer, but can you keep me updated? I need to send out some tweets."

"We?" Emily inquired, her eyebrow raised. She looked around to see if she had missed seeing someone.

"Yeah," Peter responded, "Julie's with me, although you would never know it. I promised her a ride home, but as soon as we got here, she ran up there," Peter said, pointing to the top of the bleachers.

Emily squinted to try to find her against the setting sun. "That's odd," she mused. "I actually invited her to come with us to the game today. I asked her early this morning, but she got really weird and ran off as fast as she could. I guess she likes you better!"

"Well, of course she does, who can blame her?" Peter said with a wink and a smile. "But really, she only came with me because she needs a ride home, and I get the impression that she would rather be anywhere but here right now. I told her I just wanted to check on the game before we headed out. As soon as I mentioned the game, she got squirmy." Peter glanced back in Julie's direction; she was standing up and rocking from one foot to the other. "Actually, it looks like I should probably go grab her now, before she decides to jump off the bleachers and make a run for it."

"She is actually a pretty good jumper, I've seen it with my own two eyes." Emily chuckled, thinking of Julie clearing the fence at RAWWR. "Mind if I join you two for a second before you leave?"

"Fine with me, as long as you promise to text me score updates," Peter replied.

"Deal," said Emily. "I mean, I would offer to just send the tweets out myself, but I deleted all of my social media accounts right after the fire and haven't set them up again. I guess I've been missing some pretty amazing boys' soccer updates. I wonder if anything else has happened in the past couple of months."

Peter laughed and casually grabbed her by the hand to pull her up the steps behind him. When they reached Julie, she was sitting down again, leaning into a corner of the fencing on the top of the bleachers. Her eyes were downcast, and Emily got the distinct feeling that, if it were available, Julie would have pulled the gray hat down over her face again. She just wasn't sure why.

"OK, Jules, your Uber awaits," Peter joked. "Emily here promised to update me on the score, so I'm free to go."

Julie looked up, finally seeming to realize that Emily was there. "Hey," she said quietly.

"Hey, Julie," Emily said, feeling slightly uneasy. "I just wanted to tell you that I would still love it if you stayed to hang with all of us. Nat and Sophie remember you from back in the day. They really want to get to know you again."

"Thanks," Julie replied, "but this isn't the time or the place for getting reacquainted. I would love to, though, just some other time."

Emily felt the same weird vibe that she had felt this morning. She wasn't sure if Julie had a problem with her, or Sophie and Nat, or if Julie was simply unnaturally repulsed by the game of soccer. Whatever it was, something was definitely going on. "Okay," Emily responded. "Some other time, then."

She turned to leave, but Julie had more to say. "For the record, Warren is not the golden boy that everyone thinks he is. I hope you don't hate me for saying this, but I'm only trying to protect you."

Emily turned around and headed back up the stairs toward Julie. Sometimes, she felt badly for her, but sometimes, the girl just simply pissed her off. She didn't know Julie well enough to know how to interpret what she'd just said. "I have no idea what you're talking about, Julie, but if you have something to say, I would prefer if you would just say it instead of being so damn obtuse," she hissed.

"As I said before, this is not the time or the place for the whole story, but let me start by saying this: He may be charming and pleasant on the eyes, but that's just the surface. Beyond the surface he isn't so pretty," Julie responded.

"I'm trying to be patient, here, Julie, because I like you and Jake adores you. But you're making it difficult for me to stay calm. If I were you, I would be very careful about spreading general accusations about Warren, or anyone else for that matter, unless you can back up your allegations with some specifics. For now, I'm going to head back down to watch the game. See you tomorrow. Bye, Peter, I promise to keep you posted," Emily said, wanting to get out of there as quickly as she possibly could.

But Julie stopped her again by saying, "I get it, Emily, and I have more specifics than I'm willing to share right now. Eventually, I will tell you what happened, and at that point, I hope you'll understand why I am not a huge fan of Warren's. I'm not ready to talk about it yet, but let's just start with this: Check out Warren's Instagram from the first day of school. There's a post that involves you. It's pretty mild, compared to what he did to me, but it's a good example of the kind of guy he is." Julie spoke with more passion and energy than Emily had ever heard from her before. Then, more quietly, she said, "And I honestly like you too, Emily, I don't want you getting hurt like I did."

"Ummm…thanks, I guess," she muttered, feeling increasingly agitated. "See you guys later."

She half-stomped down the stairs and back toward her place against the fence with Nat and Soph. About halfway through her descent, she looked up and noticed Warren's eyes following her. From this far away, she could not read the expression on his face. She could only see that it wasn't a pleasant one.

"Oh my goodness, what's wrong, Em?" Nat said after seeing the look on Emily's face.

"It's nothing, really. Can you pull up your Insta for me? I want to check something on Warren's page," Emily said.

"Sure. No problem," Nat said, expertly maneuvering her fingers around the touchscreen to pull up her account. She handed Emily the phone and turned her attention back to the game.

"Thanks," Emily said. "Hey. It may take a few minutes to find this. Can you text Peter if anyone scores? You can use my phone."

Emily went to work finding Warren's page and scrolling through it. It took her about ten minutes to get through the last two months of posts. Nothing really jumped out at her. There were a few recent pics of the two of them together and also some of the group at Robert's house. These were mixed in with hundreds of shared sports stories, pictures, and news briefs. Emily did notice a few not-so-flattering shots and comments as she continued investigating, but she wasn't seeing anything earth-shattering. Then, it hit her: two photos of her, taken in August. The first was the selfie Warren had taken of them on the first day of school. Emily recognized the horrible outfit she had been wearing. The second photo was one of she and Jake on the same day, from behind, walking hand in hand down the hallway. It wasn't so much the photos that were bothersome, it was the caption. Under the photos, Warren had written "#thriftstoremuch?" Emily felt instantly humiliated.

"Wow," Emily said turning to her friends and handing Nat her phone back. It was still opened to the photos. "Why didn't you guys tell me about this?"

Nat and Sophie turned away from the game and looked down at the screen. "That's so rude," Sophie said. "Why would he say something like that knowing what you guys had been through?"

"I never saw this before," Nat replied, "but I didn't start following him until we started hanging out this year. Now I'm glad I didn't. How did you know to look back to find that, Emily?"

"Julie just told me about it, along with some vague information about how she doesn't like Warren. She wouldn't give me any details, though. She said that the thrift store dig was mild compared to what he did to her."

"What does that mean?" Nat asked.

"I have no idea," Emily replied. "Just when I thought I was getting somewhere with her! I just don't get that girl. All I know is that now, I have a raging headache."

Sophie pointed to the scoreboard and said, "No doubt! Look, there are only three seconds left anyway. Let's shoot Peter a final text and get out of here."

Emily texted Peter: "*6 to 3 Brighton. Final.*" Emily didn't even bother saying good-bye to Warren.

"*Thanks for the updates. BTW RU ok???? That was a strange conversation on the bleachers,*" Peter replied immediately.

She decided she would get back to Peter later. For now, Emily's headache had quickly turned into a full-blown migraine, and it was all she could do to focus on driving home without vomiting.

So much for a relaxing afternoon. A cross-country meet might have been more enjoyable. Maybe being a typical teenager wasn't so carefree after all.

Chapter 12

Gotta Go

Last night, after the soccer game, Warren and Julie had both texted Emily. Warren had asked why she didn't stick around to see him after the game. Half-truthfully, she told him that she hadn't been feeling great. Emily's head was spinning from the vagueness of Julie's revelation and the fact that Warren had trashed her on social media. Even though Julie hadn't convinced her that Warren was the devil incarnate, she had put a small seed of doubt in Emily's mind about Warren's character. Emily needed to get to know Warren better before she decided what to make of this new information. So she put it in the back of her mind for now and gave Warren the benefit of the doubt. He hadn't even really known her that well on the first day of school, and she hoped he would never do that to her now that they were officially dating.

Julie was another story. She was persistent and maddening, but she was also believable and likable. Emily was as twisted inside about Julie as she was about Warren. If only she knew the whole story. That would add some clarity to this ridiculous situation. Julie was standing her ground, though. She texted to apologize for dumping on Emily and promised that she would be "ready" to talk to her soon. Whatever that meant. In the meantime, Emily's only choice was to go with her gut. The thing was, her gut was not quite as certain about Warren as it had been twenty-four hours ago. Seeing him today would, hopefully, solidify her feelings for him. Maybe just being close to him and feeling the energy between them was what she needed. Emily prayed that she would feel more centered once she saw him this morning. It was a really big day today, and she couldn't afford to be feeling off.

Jake had a doctor appointment that morning, so Susan had taken the day off. Even though she didn't have to walk Jake to his classroom this morning, out of habit Emily made the mistake of entering the school and heading down the hallway toward room 64. If she had been thinking about it, she would have avoided that hallway altogether this morning. She would have avoided Julie.

Once she realized her mistake, Emily tried to keep her head down and walk quickly past room 64 without being noticed. Julie seemed to be waiting for her, though. Today, she was standing, not in her usual corner, but outside of the entryway, in the actual hallway. She saw Emily coming a mile away and fell into step with her.

"Where's Jake today?" was Julie's first question. "Is he OK?"

"Yup," Emily responded, "he just has a follow-up doctor appointment. He had three heart surgeries when he was younger. The cardiologist monitors him yearly now, just to make sure his heart is growing and working as it should. He'll come to school after the appointment."

"Oh, good! I was worried there for a second," Julie said. "I just wanted to say I am sorry again, in person. I know that was bad timing. I think being at the soccer game made me feel a little anxious or something. I've been wanting to talk to you about Warren ever since you guys started getting closer. There's just never been a great time to bring it up."

"Okay," Emily said, growing more and more exasperated by the subject. "It's just that I can't really make sense of this right now. I saw the post. It was a little hurtful, granted, but we weren't really dating then, and since you aren't ready to tell me more, I just have to give him the benefit of the doubt for now. When you're ready, let me know. For today, I have a lot going on. I can't afford to be distracted by this. I have a huge meet this afternoon. Two college coaches will be there, and if I don't run well...let's just say that, given our current financial situation, my family cannot afford for me to tank today's meet. So, apology accepted. Can we move on?"

"Sure," Julie said, "for now. In any case, good luck today. I've heard that you're a talented runner."

"Thanks, Julie. Jake should be here by lunchtime, and I'm sure he will be looking for you. See you later," Emily said before heading off to class.

The rest of the day was uneventful for the most part. Emily had lunch with the regular crew. She sat next to Warren, and he held her hand for almost the entire time. It made it difficult to eat her lunch, but it felt completely natural and made Emily push the doubts she was having even further back in her mind. The only minor blip came toward the end of the lunch period. Jake returned to school and made an unusually noisy entrance when he came into the lunchroom. He excitedly greeted the friends at his lunch table, and his voice seemed exceptionally loud, carrying above most of the combined conversations in the cafeteria. Out of the corner of her eye, Emily saw Warren turn to see what the commotion was. For a brief instant, she thought she saw the expression on his face change to one of disdain. By the time he completely faced her again, his face wore its usual casual-but-confident, relaxed expression. It had happened so quickly that Emily couldn't be totally sure whether she could trust what she thought she'd seen. Once again, she buried the incident deep inside. Too much was at stake today to obsess over trivial things.

The rest of the afternoon went by slowly. When the last bell finally rang, Emily took off toward the locker room to get ready for the meet. Her archrival since seventh grade, Ellen Robbins, would be running against her today for Halston High School, and Emily had two goals: to beat her personal best time of 17:54 and to leave Ellen in her dust. Emily hoped she could get her head in a space to focus and be completely on her game. She wanted to have her best meet ever, partially because there would be two coaches scouting her but also because her father was planning on watching today.

She warmed up with the rest of the team before the race, but she tried to focus by plugging her headphones in and playing her favorite playlist. Coach didn't mind her doing this, especially before important races, as long as she warmed up exactly as she had been taught. Much like Jake, Emily loved music. It could help you focus, make you happy or sad, or give you something in common with people you'd never even met before. Music was truly magical. Emily was grateful that it did its job today. She felt focused and excited by the time she walked toward the starting line.

Emily stayed in her zone as the race began. The first 2.5 miles of the home course were always Emily's favorite, especially on a day like today. It was brisk but sunny, and there was a slight breeze blowing. Because the race was mostly through wooded areas, there were no spectators until the final half mile. The solitude she felt as she ran made her feel oddly at peace during competition. She was happy to hang behind the front runners for a little while. Once they got comfortable, she would kick it in gear.

Emily rounded the final corner in the woods and started running up the hill into the clearing. If they came to watch, that's where her mom always stood with Jake. Emily wondered which song they would sing to her today. Usually, it was one of two choices. First, it could be "Run Till You Fly." If she had to pick a favorite Dudes song, that one would be it. The second option was "Gotta Go," and though the song was appropriate for cheering her on, it was originally written to help parents when they were potty training their toddlers. As a matter of fact, it was the song Susan sang to Emily when she was two and the song they both sang to Jake for three years straight until he was finally potty trained at five-and-a-half years old. The worst part about that song was that when she heard it, to this day, it made Emily feel like she had to pee.

And, of course, that was the song Jake chose to sing as she rounded the bend. Only he wasn't singing by himself, or even just with Mom. Instead, when she emerged into the clearing, Emily saw Jake, Mom, Peter, and Julie. All four of them had their arms interlocked with one another and were jumping up and down singing happily.

You gotta go go go
We've gotta go go go
You gotta go when you gotta go

It was easy to see why Jake usually chose this song: it had fewer words and he could sing most of them. His favorite part came next, though, and Emily ran like hell to get out of there before he started singing it.

The Dudes' version of the song concluded with a child saying, "Ahhhh, that's better." Presumably, it was one of the singer's own kids. That was Jake's favorite part of the song. Once she passed by, Emily could hear him say, "Ahh..da budu budu budu budu."

In all honesty, that was the part that usually made Emily cringe, but today the sight of those four knuckleheads singing together made her smile.

Emily picked up the pace now that she was toward the latter part of the course. She put all of her energy into finishing strong and without distraction. Until she saw Warren.

Just beyond the knuckleheads, Warren stood on the edge of the trail holding a large poster above his head. Emily was momentarily touched by how sweet it was for Warren to cheer her on with a poster. Then she read it. If she hadn't been running a significant race at that very moment, she would have stopped dead in her tracks and possibly punched Warren in the face. Right now, to Warren's good fortune, that was not a choice.

Warren held a giant bright pink poster. In the middle of the poster was a photo of Emily running. Though she had never seen the photo before, she recognized that it was from the first meet of the season. The temperatures that day had approached 95 degrees in oppressive humidity. The photo was an action shot, and in it Emily was drenched in perspiration, beads of sweat flying off of her. It was not a pretty picture.

Underneath the abysmal photo, in very large, bright green letters, were the words *Don't sweat it, Emily. I'll take you to homecoming.*

Holy crap, was Emily's first thought when she saw it. *You have got to be kidding me.* She was mortified. Instantaneously, she made a decision. She let her anger drive her. She was so filled with rage and humiliation that she ran harder and faster than she had ever run before.

She ran right past two coaches with clipboards and stopwatches in hand and right past her father, who was standing directly beside them.

Best of all, she passed Ellen Robbins in the last two hundred yards of the race. Emily ran straight through the finish line and beyond. She didn't stop running until she reached the port-o-potties at the edge of the open fields.

"Gotta Go" *always* made her have to go.

When she was finished, she pushed the creaky door open and began to jog slowly back toward the finish line to greet her teammates as they came in. She was shocked to see four people running directly toward her. They were all grinning wildly.

It took a moment to register that the group consisted of her father, her coach, and the two college scouts. When they reached her, one of the scouts thrust her stopwatch in front of Emily's face. It read 17:15.

It was, by far, her personal best time ever for a three-mile

course. And in a weird way, she had Warren to thank for it.

Chapter 13

McNalley's

News of Emily's record-breaking time traveled quickly through the spectators. Emily supposed she had social media feeds to thank for that, but good old word of mouth was at work too. Before she knew it, Emily was surrounded by a mob of people offering up their congratulations. It was like a slow-motion dream. What a crazy day it had been!

The best part about the crowd was that it provided a natural human barrier between herself and Warren, so she never had to lay eyes on him after the meet. She was temporarily, yet happily, saved from responding to his ridiculous invitation. At least she had a little time to consider her options and maybe talk it over with Mom when she got home. But first, she had to survive dinner with Dad.

Survive might be a bit of an exaggeration. He wasn't that bad. Maybe *tolerate* was the word she was looking for.

Though Patrick had moved out of the house many years ago, he hadn't completely checked out of his children's lives. When he wasn't traveling for work, Emily saw him for dinner every couple of weeks. He also made it to her cross-country and track meets when he could. After Emily entered high school, Patrick actively sent photos, videos, and statistics to college coaches. He came to Jake's events too, especially Special Olympics. Oddly enough, though, he never took Jake out alone. It was like he was afraid of his own son.

Despite a tumultuous forty-eight hours, Emily was feeling pretty excited about today's race. When you have a sibling with special needs, they demand attention. Every once in a while, Emily thought, it was nice to be celebrated too.

Since Emily had driven to school, she drove herself to their usual spot at McNalley's for dinner. She blasted Thomas Rhett's new album the whole way and practically floated over to join her dad at the table. He had ordered a beer for himself and an Arnold Palmer for Emily. She was impressed that he remembered her favorite post-meet beverage.

He looked good, Emily thought as she approached their booth. Patrick was dressed in a golf shirt and khakis and, because he still had most of his hair, he looked a lot younger than his fifty-one years. Today, he looked more relaxed than she had ever seen him.

Just as she sat down, the waitress brought over a ginormous plate of nachos, a McNalley's specialty. Emily hadn't realized until that moment how ravenous she was feeling.

"It seems as though we have some things to celebrate tonight," Patrick said, "starting with my talented daughter's record-breaking time."

She blushed at the compliment and mumbled, "Thanks, Dad," through a mouth full of cheese, sour cream, and black olives. "What other things are we celebrating?"

"We'll get to that, Piglet," he replied, "but for now, I just want to relish your victory for a little while. I'm also dying to know where that fire came from today. It was like you were running from the devil himself when you came out of the woods. After dinner, I'll fill you in on the rest of the developments. I hope you'll be pleased."

Piglet had been his nickname for her ever since she was born. Though she, obviously, had no recollection of the event, both of her parents agreed that her first sound after birth was more of a snort than a cry. Patrick had found it so hilarious and endearing that he immediately went to the gift store to buy her a stuffed Piglet doll, with soft satin ears. After seventeen years, she still had that doll. Though it was tattered and dirty, Emily slept with it inside her pillowcase every night to this very day.

"So, spill it!" Patrick continued. "What in God's name was your motivation today?"

Briefly, Emily considered telling him about Warren's homecoming proposal but decided against it in the interest of keeping things light and upbeat. She never wanted this feeling of elation to end.

"I don't know," she lied. "Maybe it was the new playlist I made last night. Coach let me warm up to it today. Maybe it was the fact that I knew this was my last opportunity to impress the Providence people, or maybe it was the knuckleheads." She stifled a giggle as she pictured the four of them singing together at the edge of the woods.

"Don't think I'm familiar?" Dad said, looking confused.

"Actually, you are familiar with three of the four," Emily said, grinning. "You know Mom and Jake a little bit. Peter is another. The newest addition is Julie Wallace. She was a friend of mine in kindergarten and first grade, then she moved away. She moved back this year, and Jake is a little obsessed with her. I think Peter may like her a bit too. They've been hanging out lately. Anyway, the four of them were jumping up and down and singing to me just before I came out of the woods. Usually, I would find that distracting, but today it cracked me up."

"Well, whatever it was, keep it up." Dad laughed. "I mean, you saw me, I was standing right next to the two scouts. Pat Reynolds was acting like he had just won the damn lottery, and Donna's jaw stayed open for so long that I thought she might suck in some flies. Another meet even close to this one, and I think you'll cement a full ride to either school. I am so damn proud of you, honey."

Emily blushed again as he picked up his beer and raised it out to her. "Cheers to your brilliant future, Piglet," he said.

He really did seem to be in a fantastic mood tonight. They spent two hours there eating, drinking, and chatting easily about anything and everything. It was, quite possibly, the most comfortable Emily had felt with her dad, maybe ever.

"Dad, we'd better get the check soon," Emily said when they had finished their dessert. "We've taken up this table for way too long. Plus, I have some homework to get to."

"All right. I'll let you go, but we won't be getting a check tonight and, in the future, you can have any table you want for as long as you want in this place," Patrick said with a sheepish grin.

"What are you talking about, Dad?" Emily asked.

111

"That's one thing I wanted to celebrate with you tonight. McNalley's is mine!" Patrick said, outstretching his hand toward the center of the dining room. "It's been in the works for a while, but as of the first of the month, this place is all mine. I owe our waitress a huge tip for not blowing my cover tonight."

"What? That's amazing, Dad, but what about Levinson's?" Emily responded. Levinson's was the food distribution company that had been Patrick's employer for as long as Emily could remember.

"I left with the promise that I would now be their customer, and Mr. Levinson is 100 percent behind me. I've always dreamed of owning a restaurant. More importantly, though, it was time for me to stop spending nine out of twelve months a year traveling for work. Your mom has been through hell. You and Jake have too, and I want to be here to support all of you as much as possible. Next year, who knows where you'll be? Mom may need a second set of hands to help out with Jake when you leave. Actually, you both have probably always needed some help. I just haven't been able to give it." The mood suddenly changed as Patrick spoke. "Owning this restaurant will give me the opportunity to stay close to home to help all of you out. It will also allow me to get to know my son after all these years."

He continued, "As I said earlier this evening, I hope you consider this news worth celebrating. Oh, and one more thing," he said, reaching into his bag and grabbing an envelope. "This is for your mom. Could you give it to her? When the house burnt down, I felt so helpless. I know the insurance is going to cover the cost of rebuilding. This is to make the house just a little bit better than it was. For years, I've been looking into grants for kids with special needs. There are so many that we never qualified for before. Because of the fire, we were eligible for two grants specifically designated for improving the home environment for kids with special needs. Like, if they need a ramp or some other type equipment for accessibility. In Jake's case, I applied for money to build a sensory room onto the new house. Mr. Levinson generously agreed to match the money from the grant. As if that wasn't enough, RAWWR donated all of the proceeds from this year's walk to help with the project. It's a sizable sum, and I want your mom to know about it now, before they start rebuilding. That way, the architect can custom-design the sensory room with input from you and your mom."

And the roller coaster continues… Emily had mixed emotions about Dad being more involved in their lives than he already was. Not so much hers, but Mom's and Jake's. She was also pleasantly surprised that Dad knew enough about Jake to know that a sensory room would be a game-changer for him. She couldn't wait to start planning it out with Mom and Peter. Still, she was hesitant.

And exhausted. And overwhelmed.

As she tentatively took the envelope from her father, she didn't have the energy to ask the many questions that weighed on her heart. Instead, she asked only: "Does this mean I get free nachos for life?"

Chapter 14

Letting It Out

Emily thought about her dinner with Dad for the entire ride back to Aunt Bridget's. She had the windows open and the AC blasting fully in her face just to keep herself awake until she got home. She hoped Mom was up and waiting for her. There was so much to talk about. Despite her exhaustion, Emily didn't think she would be able to sleep until she told somebody about her day.

Thankfully, Mom was up doing the bills in Aunt Bridget's kitchen when Emily finally got home. Though she had seen her briefly after the race, she hadn't really gotten to talk to her before being caught up in the crowd of well-wishers.

Emily came up behind her mom and wrapped her arms around her, giving her a quick kiss on the cheek. She plopped down in the chair next to her and rested her head on the table. "What a day!" Emily said.

"I couldn't agree more!" Mom responded, pushing her pile of bills aside and giving Emily her full, undivided attention. "You were incredible today! I couldn't wait to talk to you about it. Waiting has been *killing* me, but I hope you had a good time with your dad."

"Mom, did you know that Dad bought McNalley's?" Emily blurted out.

Susan looked genuinely shocked. "What, wait, seriously? *The* McNalley's? F-for real?" she stammered.

"The very same," Emily replied. "He said he's worried about continuing to travel for work after I leave for college. He said he thought you and Jake might need an extra hand, so he quit Levinson's and bought McNalley's. I assumed he might have spoken to you about it."

"When I ran into him before the race today, he said he had something to discuss with me. But in all the excitement, I never actually got to see him after the race. I'll give him a call tomorrow. I know it's always been a dream of his, though. He's always wanted to own a restaurant. Maybe this will finally give him the opportunity to get to know his son," Susan said with a vague, somewhat dreamy, smile. The final sentence was barely audible, and Emily wondered if her mom had intended to say it out loud.

"That's what I thought! I only wish he'd wanted to know Jake from the beginning. What kind of father leaves his child?" Emily exclaimed.

"Now, Emily, it's not quite as simple as that," Susan rebuked, "Your father has wrestled with this for many years. He's supported us financially and has tried to be involved to the level he felt comfortable. We have done OK, and I forgave him for walking out long ago. He's right about one thing, though: I will need some extra help. Losing you and Peter at the same time is going to sting."

It was only then that Emily noticed that there was music coming from the living room. "Is Peter here now?" she asked.

"Yes, with that lovely Julie Wallace. They're working on a 'special project.' Apparently it's top secret and neither of us can know what it is," Susan said.

"Julie's here, too?" Emily asked.

"For about ten more minutes. I told the conspirators that Jake has almost had enough. I'm kicking them out at nine," Susan replied.

"Well, then, can I use that ten minutes to get some advice?" Emily pleaded.

Susan looked her gently in the eye. "Of course, my love. I always have time for you."

Emily was surprised to feel hot tears streaming down her face before she even started talking.

"Baby! What's the matter? Is everything OK?" Susan said, startled.

"Yeah, no, I don't know, Mom. So much has happened over the past two days that I can't even begin to process it. Dad, Julie, Warren, the race. I'm totally wiped out. But, since I only have ten minutes until Jake's bedtime, I guess I want to start with Warren. But for you to understand what's going on with Warren, I need to fill you in on what happened with Julie yesterday. I guess I'd better talk fast. I'm already down to nine minutes," Emily choked out.

As quickly as possible, Emily summarized Julie's behavior from the soccer game and the vague references to something Warren had done to her. In the interest of time, she left out many of the details, including the Instagram post and the look she thought she had seen from Warren at lunch today. If she had even hinted about the look, Susan would have turned full-blown protective "Mama Bear" on her. That would make it harder for her to be objective about the next part.

Emily concluded with the homecoming proposal at the race today. She was so embarrassed that she couldn't even look away from her own hands on the table until she got through the story. Only when she finished did she dare to look up at her mother's face. Susan's mouth was open. She made several attempts to try to speak before she was actually successful.

"Wow!" she finally managed. "Well, first off, I just want to say that it's totally understandable that you're feeling overwhelmed. That's so much to process, even for me. I can't imagine what you've been going through!" She took a deep breath. "I guess the first question I want to ask is, how well do you know Warren? What's your gut feeling? Have you ever felt unsafe or threatened by him?"

"No! Not at all, Mom!" Emily replied. "If I did, I wouldn't be hanging out with him. I feel really happy when I'm around him. I haven't known him for that long, but I do trust him. Or at least I did...until yesterday."

Susan listened intently and said, "You're a good kid. You've never given me any trouble. You've always acted maturely...maybe you had to grow up faster than other kids because of having to be more responsible and independent. Maybe it's just good genetics. Either way, the point is that I trust you. I trust you to make your decision based on what you know and what you feel. We would all be in a lot of trouble if we only allowed ourselves to have relationships that were approved by others. If you're truly happy with Warren, then you should stay happy. If and when Julie chooses to share her secret with you, you're free to change your mind."

Emily nodded as Susan continued, "That being said, there's one thing that I do know about Warren."

"What?" Emily asked.

"That boy has a lot to learn about romance," her mom said. "'Don't sweat it!' That is so ridiculous, it's actually funny."

"I *know*, right?" Emily choked out. She started laughing hysterically thinking about it.

Right on cue, Peter walked Jake into the kitchen at nine. They both looked tired and happy. "What's so funny?" Peter asked, looking at Emily.

"It's a long story! I promise to fill you in later," Emily said as she grabbed Jake's hand and led him toward the staircase. "For now, 'Jake's Nighttime Dream Show' is about to begin, and it's my turn to put this guy to bed. Good night, everyone! Oh, and by the way, Mom, Dad wanted me to give you that envelope on the table. It's something for the new house."

Ten minutes later, Emily heard a loud "Woo-hoo!" coming from downstairs. Despite the craziness of the day, it made her heart feel light.

Chapter 15

Do You Wanna Dance?

After putting Jake to bed and getting herself ready, Emily was still feeling exhausted but unsettled. She FaceTimed with Nat and Sophie so that she could get their perspective on Warren's homecoming proposal. If she didn't talk about it, it drove her crazy, and if she didn't laugh about it, it made her entire face burn with embarrassment. Thank goodness not many people had been around to see it.

For the most part, Sophie and Nat echoed her mother's sentiments: that it was too early to cut ties with Warren if that decision was based solely on somebody else's very nonspecific opinion. But they also agreed that, if the decision was being made based on his complete lack of basic common sense, then she had their full support. In the end, she decided that all might be forgiven if she could just stare into his hypnotic blue eyes for an entire evening. Like, at homecoming, for example. She texted him to tell him that she would go with him on one condition: that he destroy the poster and promise to never ever display that picture in public again. Although he agreed, he seemed a little insulted at the request.

Thankfully, the latter part of the week was more low- key than the first two days. Things kind of went back to a peaceful routine. Emily saw Warren in class and at lunch, and they talked a lot in the evenings when things settled down. When they were one-on-one, she was beginning to like him a lot, but when everything was too quiet in her mind, a persistent, nagging doubt slithered its way into her consciousness.

After Tuesday's personal record-breaking run, Emily was happy to have a few days to just practice before the weekend invitational meet on Saturday. Her practice runs were decent, though nothing close to the time she had run earlier in the week. On one or two occasions, she even tried to conjure the feeling of rage she had felt after seeing Warren's poster. That magnitude of emotion, unfortunately, was hard to fake.

On the way home from practice on Friday, Emily was deeply focused on Saturday's meet. The downside of Tuesday's run was the expectation that she had the ability to easily do it again. Emily had spent a lot of time in the past few days considering what kind of times she could manage on her own merit, without an emotional catalyst. It was making her more nervous to run than she had been in a very long while.

Her plan, for tonight, was to take a shower, grab dinner, talk to Warren, and head to bed early to get a good night's sleep. That, at least, she could control. She was met with an unexpected scene when she pulled down the driveway to Aunt Bridget's house. She brought her Jeep to a stop, got out, walked to the passenger side, and leaned against it, watching it unfold.

Jake was standing on the large brick landing that led to the front door, dancing and smiling. The door was open, and Aunt Bridget and her mom looked on from just inside the door. Julie and Peter stood on the walkway, dancing in sync and holding a giant poster above their heads. It looked like they were doing the twist. Next to Julie was a Bluetooth speaker, playing the 1950s Bobby Freeman song "Do You Wanna Dance?" From the looks of it, Jake did.

Until that moment, Emily had forgotten about that song. it was one of the few non-kid songs that Jake loved, and he loved it because of their dad. Briefly, an image flashed in Emily's head of the three of them dancing to this song in the old living room. Jake must have been about three or four, and Dad held him in one arm as he danced around the room holding Emily's hand. Emily could vividly remember the smile on Jake's face and how it mirrored the one that her dad wore that day.

Curious, but not wanting to disturb the happy vibe of the moment, Emily quietly crept down the driveway. She wanted to find a vantage point that would allow her to see what the poster said, while staying outside of Jake's line of vision. She managed to find a safe spot and peered at the sign. Not surprisingly, it said, "Hey, Jake, do you want to dance?" Because Jake could not read, there were picture symbols underneath the words "Jake," "you," "want," and "dance." Emily drew a breath in as she realized it was a homecoming proposal for Jake from Peter and Julie. What an amazing thing for them to do for him.

"Oh my goodness!" she gasped to herself. "That's awesome!" To her best recollection, nobody had ever done anything like that for Jake. Though she was incredibly impressed, she also felt strangely like an outsider in that moment. She stood still for a few minutes, absorbing the scene.

When the song ended, Jake signed "more" and shouted, "Ma...ma...ma...ge!" Ever since Emily could remember, when Jake was very excited about something, asking for "more" was never enough. Jake used "more" when he was asking for mundane things, like more Goldfish crackers or mashed potatoes. When he was super-excited, he added "more" and "again" together, as he had in this situation.

"Yeah, buddy!" Peter said, giving Jake an exuberant fist bump. Julie whispered something to Peter, and he nodded in agreement. He reached to grab the phone out of his back pocket to play the song again.

Just then, Emily noticed she had been spotted. Julie skipped over and grabbed Emily's hand. "I was hoping you would be here!" she said. "Come join the party."

Emily agreed. She followed Julie to where Peter stood and, standing between the two of them, held the sign over her head. When the music started again, the six of them did the twist together on the front lawn in front of Aunt Bridget's house.

Emily smiled, thinking about how spontaneous dance parties often broke out when Jake was around. She silently wondered how many times things like this happened at other people's houses, concluding that they probably almost never did. *Another advantage to having Jake for a sibling,* she thought.

When the music stopped, Susan offered to make burgers for everyone. They all happily accepted.

"Wait!" Peter said. "Jake, you haven't given us an answer yet! What do you think? Do you want to go to the dance? Yes...or...no?"

Peter added the choice of yes or no while speaking slowly and signing both words. He knew what a hard time Jake had understanding questions without some kind of visual input. Giving him the choice always cued him in to the fact that a response was expected of him.

"Ya!" Jake responded with a fist pump in the air. Everyone laughed and followed Susan and Bridget to the back patio for an impromptu cookout.

"Now *that* is what I call a promposal!" Emily said.

"We actually think of it more as a 'songposal,'" Peter laughed.

"Either way, you two could teach Warren a thing or two about how to do this right!" Emily said.

"What do you mean?" Peter asked, looking a little confused. "Come on, spill it, Em."

Emily found herself desperate to tell Peter everything as soon as Julie was out of earshot. She didn't really want to stir anything up tonight. When Julie went inside with Susan to help, Emily turned to face Peter and quickly relayed the story of Warren's disastrous idea of

126

a homecoming proposal. Now that she'd had several days to come to terms with it, she was now able to relay the story with a lighthearted and amused undertone. Peter's response was uproarious laughter.

"You're kidding, right? That guy is seriously a piece of work!" Peter said when he was able to breathe again.

Emily nodded in agreement, but her eyes never left his face. "And yet, I agreed to go," she responded with an exaggerated roll of her eyes.

"Someday, I will have to ask you to a dance myself. Just so you can experience the kind of proposal you truly deserve," Peter said more seriously.

"Awww. That's the sweetest, Peter. But I think you just showed me how it's supposed to be done."

"Yeah, I did!" Peter responded, with feigned smugness that was not at all a true part of who he was.

Julie returned carrying a giant salad, which was one of Aunt Bridget's specialties. She set it down on the table and sat down on the other side of Peter on the bench. Susan and Aunt Bridget followed closely behind. They each grabbed a burger and some sides, said grace, and dug in.

"Hey, Ms. P," said Peter with a mouth full of burger, "Julie and I have a question for you."

"I'll make you a deal, Peter. I agree to answer your question, but only after you swallow." Susan laughed.

Peter obliged and wiped his mouth with a napkin before he continued, "Sorry, Ms. P. I just got a little excited about this idea. I'm not sure if you know it or not, but Julie and I are doing the play. They are doing *Days Bright with Laughter* this year. It's a newer musical. They just had auditions. I was going for one of the leads, but I got a smaller, supporting role and an understudy to the lead, which they gave to Nathan Hawkings. Julie is helping backstage and with the set. We were wondering if Jake could come with us, after school, to rehearsals. I don't have many lines, so I will be pretty free to watch him. I think he would love the music, and we may even be able to find a small role for him. Plus, Julie and I are working on something special for him. What do you think? Maybe Emily could bring him home after practice or meets and save you a trip sometimes."

Julie nodded in agreement the entire time Peter spoke.

Susan smiled. "Wow. I love that idea, Peter. Thank you for offering. Let me give some thought to the logistics and talk it over with Em. I honestly have been meaning to get him signed up for something so that he's able to do more than just school and therapy, but it's been really hard since the fire. I've always thought that, with his endless facial expressions, Jake was born to be on stage. I do have to ask you if you know what you're getting into, though. I mean, you know Jake in his home environment, and I don't think he will give you any trouble, but you never know how he'll react to new experiences and changes in his routine."

"I get it, Ms. P," Peter replied. "I've known Jake for a long time. I eat lunch with him every day, and we see each other at school sometimes. How about we give it a shot on a trial basis? Let's say a week or so? If it doesn't seem to be working or if he doesn't seem to be enjoying it, we can definitely revisit the plan. Think about it this way, having Jake to entertain will help me get over the sting of losing the starring role to Nathan Hawkings again." Peter made a slight gagging gesture as he said the name. "That guy can't even sing!"

Susan smiled. "A trial run seems like a good idea. Let me see if any familiar staff are involved with drama. I'll send Mrs. Lawrence a quick text and then we can work out the details."

"Rehearsals start in a few weeks, so we have until then to figure it out!" Peter replied.

Susan turned to Emily. "How does that sound to you, Em?" she asked, but her question was met only with the soft, rhythmic sounds of Emily's breathing as she slept quietly, her head resting on the table.

Susan stifled a laugh. "Looks like Emily's week has taken a toll on her. I'm just happy she moved her plate out of the way before she fell asleep! I guess I'll walk her up to bed now. She should try to get a good night's sleep—she has the invitational tomorrow morning."

Jake jumped up and repetitively thumped his chest with one hand. "Ma! Ma! Ma! Ma!" he said, looking at Emily.

"OK, Jake. Great idea. This time, you get to help Emily up to bed," Susan said.

As Jake gently guided Emily up the stairs, he could not have looked prouder.

And Peter found himself unable to look away.

Chapter 16

The Chicken Dance

The next two weeks passed quickly in a whirlwind of school, meets, life, and one of Emily's favorite things: shopping! By some miracle Sophie, Nat, and Emily were able to find time the Saturday before homecoming to shop for dresses. By an even greater miracle, they were able to convince Julie to come with them. Emily was happy that Julie agreed to go, even though the event didn't include Peter or Jake. She was a little apprehensive, though, that Julie might take the opportunity to finally decide that she was "ready" to discuss her history with Warren.

As it turned out, the day was fantastic. They each found the perfect shoes, dresses, and accessories. It was one of those magical shopping days where everything fell into place. They even had time to grab a bite at McNalley's before heading home. Patrick was there, and he came to sit with them for a few minutes. He seemed happy and relaxed despite the fact that the bar was packed and the restaurant was virtually overflowing with customers.

Patrick stayed only a few minutes and made small talk with the girls before standing up abruptly to leave the table.

"Come on, Dad! You're the boss, can't you stay a little longer?" Emily whined.

Patrick cleared his throat, looking suddenly uncomfortable. He lifted his eyes and spoke softly to Emily. "Actually, Piglet, I have to go grab Jake. I'm taking him suit shopping this afternoon. I understand he got quite the invitation to homecoming."

Emily noted Julie's smile in response to the subtle compliment even as she tried to mask her own surprise.

"Wow, Dad. I didn't know that. You'd better get going, then. Jake hates to wait. I am sure he's driving Mom nuts asking when you will be there," Emily said.

Patrick laughed and replied, "You know him so well, I'm sure you're right, and Em, I'm really looking forward to doing more with Jake from now on."

He gave Emily a quick kiss on the cheek and turned to go. She watched him give a few orders to the head waiter and to the hostess before he grabbed his jacket and walked out the door. He was certainly surprising her these days. When he had gone, Emily turned her attention back to her friends at the table.

132

"I'm never going to fit into the dress I just bought if I keep eating like this," Nat was saying.

Julie laughed and said, "Me neither, but at least we have almost a week to work it off. Seriously, you guys, thanks for including me today. I had more fun than I've had in a long time."

"No problem, Julie," said Nat. "Hey, why don't we see if they can squeeze Julie in at the salon next Saturday for our hair appointments?"

"If they can't she could always just wear her gray hat," joked Emily.

Sophie and Nat looked at each other; they seemed to be wondering if it was a little too soon to joke about that. But Julie responded by laughing so hard she spit her soda all over her T-shirt.

"Sorry to disappoint you, Emily, but I already threw that thing out," said Julie. "I don't think I'll be needing it anymore."

As it turned out, Julie's gray hat was completely unnecessary for homecoming. Emily was stunned to see how beautiful Julie looked and how complete her transformation had been in just a few weeks' time. At the salon, they had decided to leave her hair long and wavy, with just the front pulled away from her face. As she got out of her car in Aunt Bridget's driveway, her blond hair blew in the breeze. She looked like a model in her emerald-green dress. Julie had opted to stop by just for pictures right before she, Peter, and Jake were scheduled to leave. Emily assumed it was to minimize any possible interaction with Warren. She gave Julie credit for coming at all but was still confused about what had happened. She had even broached the subject with Warren a couple of days ago, but he swore up and down that he had never done anything to hurt Julie.

Everyone besides Julie had come to Aunt Bridget's earlier in the afternoon for snacks and drinks. She had set up a small feast for them on the patio, and they were all enjoying the food and sunshine while they snapped and posted pictures. When Julie rounded the corner and walked toward the group, Emily noticed EJ, Robert, and Peter momentarily gawking at her before collecting their composure again. Warren, on the other hand, moved to the opposite end of the table and avoided eye contact completely as he played with his leftover taco dip. It was very obvious that something had happened between them and that Warren knew exactly what it was.

Because Susan was aware of the tension between Warren and Julie, and because she was ever the diplomat, she quickly gathered the kids for a group photograph as soon as Julie came into view. She was careful to arrange them so that Warren and Julie were separated, but she did want Emily and Jake to be next to each other. She placed Nat, EJ, Soph, Robert, and Warren to the right. She then put Emily in the middle with Jake, Peter, and Julie to her left. Warren and Peter handed Susan their phones, promising to share the photos with everyone else. As quickly as possible, Susan snapped a few pictures, gave the phones back, and said good-bye to Jake, Peter, and Julie. Susan watched with a smile as the three of them pulled away in Peter's car. Mrs. Anderson, Jake's school aide, was one of the chaperones and would be at the dance just in case. Hopefully, that would keep Jake out of trouble.

Robert's father had provided his personal limo for Robert and his friends. To Emily, it seemed a little over the top to take a limo to homecoming, but everyone else seemed good with it. If she had learned anything from being friends with Robert, it was that pretty much everything his family did was a little over the top. Who was she to turn down a free limo ride?

Robert's father had stocked the limo with snacks, soda, and sparkling cider. After Aunt Bridget's pre-homecoming feast, nobody was hungry, but they quickly popped the cork on the cider and poured everyone a glass. Warren released Emily's hand only to take a few more pictures.

"I just posted the photos from Emily's house, guys. Check them out!" Warren said.

Since the fire, Emily had continued to use her phone only for necessary communication and GPS, so she had decided just to leave it home. She didn't even want to bother keeping track of it at the dance. There were plenty of phones around in case of an emergency. So, she leaned over Nat's shoulder to take a look at the pictures on her feed.

"These are amazing! We look *hot*!" Nat giggled. "Seriously, though, guys, for a bunch of hard-core athletes, we clean up good!"

Everyone nodded in agreement and scrolled through the rest of their feeds to see everyone else's pre-homecoming pictures. But something about their picture was nagging at Emily. "Hey, Nat, can I see our picture again?" she asked.

"Sure, just a sec," Nat said. "Let me just finish this comment on Nathan's photo." She paused for a second or two while she typed. "Here you go." She handed Emily the phone and went back to her cider.

Emily scrolled back to Warren's post from her house, trying to figure out what it was that hadn't seemed quite right on first glance. Once she saw it again, it was pretty obvious. Peter had posted the same photo as Warren. Everyone looked amazing, including Jake in his new suit. In Warren's post, though, only six of them were visible. He had cropped the photo so that Emily was the last one on the left side, leaving out Jake, Peter, and Julie. Given the mystery of their relationship, Emily sort of understood why Warren would want to crop Julie out of the picture, but why Jake and Peter? As she handed Nat's phone back, that familiar unsettled feeling washed over her again. As she had so many times in the past two weeks, she brushed it off and painted a smile on. She was determined to have fun with Warren tonight.

And she did. It was a perfect, magical night—up until it wasn't. The DJ was phenomenal and managed to play every request at just the right time, keeping the energy of the room high and happy. Emily was not surprised to learn firsthand that Warren was a confident and amazing dancer. A lot of the guys chose to sit out the fast songs, but Warren and Emily stayed on the floor for almost the entire night. Sometimes they danced together, and sometimes they danced in a big group. During the slower songs, Emily was not aware of anyone else on the floor. It felt like they were the only ones in the room as Warren held Emily close and sang softly in her ear. When he did that, it melted Emily's heart and made her legs feel weak. She was grateful for his strong arms around her, holding her tight. Her confusion and misgivings melted away minute by minute as the evening passed.

Toward the end of the night, the DJ made a call for last requests. Within thirty seconds of that announcement, Emily felt a hard slap on the back of her shoulder. She turned around to see Jake, jumping excitedly behind her. It was the first time she had spoken with him since they'd left Aunt Bridget's house, although she had been silently peeking over throughout the night to make sure that he was behaving. She knew Mrs. Anderson was keeping a watchful eye on him from the periphery, but it just settled her to check in on him too.

"Hey, Jake. What's up?" Emily said as she turned away from Warren's embrace. Fortunately, as she looked at his face, she could easily tell that he was happy.

"Ba ba ba!" Jake said, gesturing to the DJ.

Warren gave an exasperated sigh. "He wants to play ball *now*?" he said to Emily.

"Give me a second to figure out what he's trying to tell me," she responded. Emily conjured up as much patience as she could, telling herself that Warren did not know Jake very well, if at all.

"Ba ba ba!" Jake said, more loudly now, while he pinched his index finger and thumb together in front of his lips. Emily recognized the sign for "bird." Out of the corner of her eye, Emily could see Warren take a few steps backward, distancing himself from her and Jake.

"Sure, Jake, let's go ask the DJ to play the Chicken Dance!" Emily said, smiling. She turned to grab Warren's hand and pull him back toward her, thinking he would accompany them to make the request. "It's OK, Warren. He doesn't want to play ball, he just wants the DJ to play the Chicken Dance. It's one of his favorites. Come on. Let's go help him ask."

Warren abruptly pulled his hand away and shoved it in his pocket. "*The Chicken Dance?* Seriously? You have got to be kidding. That song is so stupid!" he said. Then he looked her in the eyes, his expression softening, and said, "Can you bring him back to Peter now so I can have you all to myself for a little while longer?"

Jake didn't always understand words, but he was a master of comprehending body language, and he knew that Warren was not thrilled with his presence. He stared down at the gym floor.

Emily felt momentarily stunned by Warren's attitude but quickly got her wits about her again. "I'll be back after we go talk to the DJ," she said as she grabbed Jake by the hand. "Come on, buddy, let's go see if he'll play your song."

As they made their way up to the stage, Jake skipped beside her. They approached the DJ's assistant, who bent down toward Jake. "How're you doing, buddy? Do you have a request?" she asked. Emily was impressed that she addressed Jake directly rather than looking helplessly toward Emily to be the translator.

"Ba ba ba," Jake said, making the chicken sign again. "Ba ba ba!"

"OK," she replied. "Is it a song about a bird?"

Jake nodded his head emphatically and said, "Ba ba!"

"Think weddings and chickens," Emily whispered discreetly into her ear. She wanted Jake to feel successful and independent in his communication, but without his talker to clarify his speech, it was a lot tougher.

"Young man, would you like to hear the Chicken Dance?" asked the assistant.

"Ya!" Jake replied, jumping up and down and clapping his hands.

"Coming right up! I have a little pull with the DJ up there, so I'm going to ask him to put that song on right away!" she said as she looked at Emily with a sly wink. "I have a feeling that patience isn't his strong suit, am I right?"

"You hit the nail on the head!" Emily replied, laughing. Then she turned to Jake. "Let's go dance with Julie and Peter. What do you say?"

Jake didn't have to say anything; he just took off running toward Peter. Emily had no hope of following him in heels, so she kicked them off and walked behind at a brisk pace, keeping a watchful eye on him. When he was safely back with his crew, she scanned the room looking for Warren. She wanted to tell him that she would be back after the next song. He wasn't where she had left him. Instead, he was in the very back of the gym, near the door, staring daggers toward Jake. She wasn't sure if he knew that she saw him or not, but she made a beeline toward Peter, Julie, Jake, and their group. She wasn't so interested in talking to Warren at the moment.

The assistant handed the DJ a note. Emily saw him chuckle a bit as he read it. He grabbed the mic and said, "Our next request is one that I don't often get at homecoming, but, according to my lovely assistant, it comes from a very enthusiastic young man. So pull out your chicken wings and get ready to shake your butt. I think you're gonna have some fun with this one!"

With that, he played Jake's request. Some of the kids looked a little confused and walked away, but the majority stayed on the floor and joined in. Even some of the guys that had held up the wall for the entire night came out with giant smiles on their faces. Nat, Sophie, EJ, and Robert came to join Jake's group at some point during the song. Warren, on the other hand, was nowhere in sight. His demeanor had done a complete 180 in the past ten minutes.

Emily faced Jake directly as the music played. Jake was totally in his element. He knew every move to that song and sang the silly words to the best of his ability. Peter and Julie were on the opposite side of Emily, and they were both totally absorbed in the contagiousness of Jake's delight. By the end of the song, Emily's face hurt from laughing for four straight minutes, and her heart felt light from the childlike, carefree spirit that her brother exuded during these times. When she finally looked up, she was totally amazed that their small group was encircled by a giant, smiling, wing-flapping mob.

Emily was shocked to discover that Jake was the literal center of attention. She was actually so surprised that she stepped back quickly, tripping over the shoes that she had dropped behind her while she was chasing Jake. She stumbled a bit, but, before she could fall, Peter's arms were around her, helping to steady her. Emily blushed with embarrassment, but Peter quickly put her at ease. "Can you *believe* this, Em? It's so cool! Look how happy Jake is, and look how happy he makes everyone else." Peter's eyes flashed with genuine amazement.

Leave it to Peter to almost effortlessly turn her attention from her own self-absorption to something much more important in the grand scheme of things. "It's crazy, right?" she replied, matching his excitement. Every once in a while, it was nice to see people appreciating Jake's gifts, even if they didn't realize it.

When the song was over, a bunch of Jake's "morning" friends came over to see him. He stood in place for a solid two minutes, giving everyone that passed a high five or a fist bump. He was in his glory. Emily just watched the scene unfold with a rare feeling of pride. It was like being an extra in a well-choreographed scene from a Hollywood movie.

At the end of the line of admirers, Emily finally saw Warren moving toward them. In complete contrast to the rest of the crowd, he scowled as he walked past Jake, neither acknowledging him nor returning his high five. Emily could see disappointment flickering in Jake's eyes.

Warren was focused on something completely different. "Dude! Do you want to take your hands off my girlfriend?" he snapped.

Until that moment, Emily was unaware that Peter's hand was still resting on the small of her back. He pulled it away quickly, making Emily think that Peter had also forgotten that it was there.

"Sorry, 'dude,'" Peter said with uncharacteristic sarcasm, "I was just trying to help the lady out."

Emily didn't even feel the need to explain herself to Warren, but she was taken aback, yet again, by his attitude. It was like he was completely jealous and insecure. What got her the most, though, was his complete lack of respect for Jake as a human being. Internally, she was fuming. She made a decision right then and there that if Warren didn't have the heart to accept or at the very least acknowledge her brother, he didn't really have a place in her life. It broke her heart into pieces to think that an evening that began so beautifully could have ended on such a sour note.

Of course, Warren could not have known that the events of the night had given Emily a sad clarity about the future of their relationship. He turned to her, softening his expression again. He grabbed her hand just as the DJ was announcing the final song of the night.

"Come on, Emily," he said. "Can I please have one more dance?"

Emily nodded in agreement and reluctantly followed him back out onto the floor, her thoughts racing.

As she was led away from the crowd, she could feel Peter's eyes following her, probably questioning what the heck she saw in this guy. Right now, Emily wondered the same, but she figured she would clarify that with Peter later, if given the chance. One thing was for sure: Warren had no idea that this dance would, literally, be the last. At least for now.

Chapter 17

Ready Now

Breaking up with Warren did not exactly go as planned, but least it was done. Emily silently considered their final conversation as she rode home in the back of Peter's car. Warren was a complicated blend of confident and cool combined with clueless and insecure. In a single night, Emily had realized what a frustrating mix that could be in a boyfriend.

She had expected that when she broke up with him, he would be pissed, at the very least. Instead, his reaction made him seem like a broken child. He didn't even appear all that surprised, maybe just a little regretful.

After the last dance at homecoming, Emily had pulled Warren into the lobby so that they could have some privacy. She chose her words carefully because when it was just the two of them, they were great together. It was the rest of the world that challenged their relationship a little too much. Emily explained to Warren that Jake was a huge part of her life, just as any sibling would be, but even more. She truthfully admitted that she liked him a lot but that she felt that their relationship could never move forward if he didn't accept Jake. She and Jake were far too interconnected.

To her utter shock, Warren didn't argue. Rather, he deflated right in front of her eyes, leaving no sign of the popular young man she thought she was dating. "You're right," he had agreed. "I guess I never thought that dating you would mean kind of dating Jake too. Maybe if I knew him better, I would feel more comfortable with him. He just makes me nervous—I don't know how to act around him. It's worth it to me to learn, though. You're worth it to me. I'll find a way to prove it to you."

In the end, they had agreed to take a break for a while to see how things played out. As she walked through the parking lot after the dance, her throat was thick with a mixture of relief, regret, and hope that someday it could still work out. She continued contemplating all of the events of the evening for the entire ride home.

Peter and Julie escorted her and Jake to the door of Aunt Bridget's house. As expected, Susan was waiting for them in the living room, sipping chamomile tea and wearing her lavender panda bear pajamas. Her hair was up in a crazy ponytail, and she looked like a teenager herself. Emily felt incredibly grateful for her mom.

"Come on in, everyone! I want to hear everything!" she said.

Jake sat right down on Susan's lap and rested his head on her shoulder, looking like an oversized toddler. It was an amusing scene given that Jake probably outweighed Susan by twenty pounds. She encircled him with her arms and gave him a tender kiss on the top of his head.

"Hold those thoughts!" she whispered. "I want to hear about it, but it looks like Jake is partied out. Let me get him to bed and then you can dish."

As usual, Jake had another opinion. "Ha, up," he said sleepily, pointing to Julie. "Ha" was Jake's name for Julie, since day one when he had spotted her in the corner. She could cut the hat apart and burn all the pieces, but to Jake she would always be "Gray Hat." To Jake, first impressions were often set in stone.

"Sure, Jake," Julie replied somewhat nervously, "lead the way!"

Peter jumped to Julie's rescue. "Mind if I come too, Jake? I can show Julie where to find your song." Jake nodded in response as he rubbed his eyes and stumbled off Susan's lap. Together, they escorted Jake to bed.

Taking advantage of a little time alone with her mom, Emily shared her version of the night's events, from the limo ride to the Chicken Dance and the breakup. She was surprised that, though her heart was heavy, she did not shed a single tear as she spoke.

"Wow!" Susan replied, reaching out to grab Emily's hand. "I'm so sorry, Emily. In life, there are a lot of ignorant people, especially when it comes to anything that's different from what they know. I'm just sorry that Warren had to be one of them. He probably hasn't had any experience with individuals with special needs. I'm also proud at the maturity and selflessness you've shown. Your brother is a lucky young man."

"But, Mom," Emily responded, "I'm so conflicted. I know that it was the right thing to do, but I also really like him. It's like he's two different people. Every once in a while, his flaws are blatant, but he's really not a bad guy…"

"You're absolutely right, Emily," choked Julie from behind them, tears running down her face. "He's not a 'bad' guy at all. He's so much worse than bad. He's a self-absorbed SOB. He's pure evil. 'Bad' doesn't do him justice!"

Peter perched himself on the fireplace hearth as Julie pulled her phone out of her purse, searching for something as she spoke. "It's time I told you guys the truth. Now seems to be as good a time as any."

She handed Emily the phone. The screen was damp with tears, but underneath Emily deciphered a startling image. It was a photo, but it contained no faces, just a hand resting against a naked breast. Underneath the photo were two captions: #Juliesback, #gettingreacquainted.

Emily gasped and looked from Julie to her mom and back. Julie nodded, and Emily handed the phone to her mom so she could see.

"That's my Instagram, and that's me…and Warren's hand. Only I didn't post it, he did." Emily paused for a moment, sobbing. Susan placed a hand on her back, trying to comfort her. Emily just sat there silently, trying to process what everything meant.

"On our second day back in town, my mom ran into Robert's mom at the supermarket. She remembered my mom, and they struck up a conversation. She mentioned that Robert was having a get-together at their beach house that night and suggested that I come. If I've learned anything from our frequent moves, it's that you have to push yourself through awkward moments at the beginning to make the year successful. So I did. I went to the party. Since I didn't know anyone in town anymore, I went solo. No matter how many times I do that, it always sucks at first. It's just completely awkward. Anyway, when I got there, Robert's mom introduced me to everyone. After that, I was on my own."

She took a deep breath and continued, "So there was a keg there and really no adult supervision whatsoever. I had a drink or two in the hot sun to help me loosen up and feel more comfortable making conversation with virtual strangers. It did the trick, but I completely regret it now. Warren and I hit it off really well. We played volleyball, and we sat and talked about a lot of things: what we remembered about each other, what I had been doing since I left, what he had been doing, hopes for the future. Everything. I was actually having a blast.

"When it got dark, we all sat around a big bonfire. Warren and I had another drink. I was honestly having a great time getting reacquainted with everyone, playing games, and posting pictures. At some point late in the evening, I passed out next to Warren on a beach lounger. My phone was still unlocked and in my hand. That's when Warren must have pulled down my bikini top and taken the picture. But because this was posted from my own account, there's no way I can prove that I wasn't a willing participant in this.

"When I woke up, I was in a panic. Warren was sleeping next to me on the lounger. I had a midnight curfew, so I immediately picked up the phone to see what time it was. As soon as I looked at the screen, I noticed that there were hundreds of notifications. I assumed they were related to the posts from the beach and the bonfire, but when I clicked on my account, I saw that." She gestured toward the phone.

"Of course, I deleted it immediately, but the damage had already been done, especially to me and my reputation. The post had already been seen or liked a bunch of times before I even woke up. Who knows how many more people saw it"—Julie choked back a sob and wiped her nose on her sleeve—"or screen-shotted it. I still don't even want to think about that, but I know the photo is still out there and that my name is on it. The comments were ruthless and unforgiving, and it made me never want to show my face in this town again. And that warm welcome back to Brighton was brought to me compliments of your good friend, Warren. Since that night, he's never even had the balls to acknowledge my presence, much less apologize."

Susan had put her arms around Julie as she spoke. Emily just sat silently, trying to reconcile this story with the Warren that she knew. Warren was sweet and thoughtful, but he could also be just plain oblivious. And he didn't seem to have a single cruel bone in his body as far as she could tell. The story just didn't add up even though the proof was on the screen right in front of her.

"How do you know for sure this is Warren's hand? How do you know that he did this, and not somebody else?" Emily asked.

Susan shot Emily a glare over the top of Julie's head, but Emily's brain was buzzing, and she needed to get the facts straight in her head. She looked at the picture again. Honestly, if Warren had been sleeping too, it could have been anybody that did this to Julie. "I'm sorry, don't get me wrong," Emily said. "What happened to you was absolutely horrible. I can't even imagine what you have been going through. I just don't understand how you know that Warren was responsible."

"I know you don't want to accept it, but it was Warren. I know it," Julie said with certainty, her tear-filled eyes meeting Emily's. "If you look closely, you'll see a faint letter on the hand. The rest of the hand is tan, but the letter 'J' is lighter. Can you see it?" Julie paused while Emily, Susan, and Peter looked at the picture again.

Peter turned away, looking pale.

"Yes, I can see it," Emily replied weakly, not really wanting to learn the significance. She assumed the letter, somehow, directly incriminated Warren.

"I told you how Warren and I hung out for most of the day, right?" Julie asked.

The three of them nodded in response.

"When I was first reintroduced to Warren, he kept forgetting my name. Actually, he kept thinking I was Vanessa White. Apparently, she also moved away in first or second grade. He must have called me Vanessa twenty-five times before I took my sunscreen stick and wrote a 'J' on his hand. I figured he wouldn't forget me if the first letter of my name was temporarily tattooed on his hand by the sun."

Julie's voice faded. Emily could tell she was exhausted.

"That's how I know it was him," she concluded before collapsing next to Peter on the hearth. He quickly put his arm around her to comfort her, and she buried her head in his shoulder and murmured, "Thank you."

Susan was the first to speak. "Julie, that was so incredibly brave. Did you tell anyone else about this? Your mom? The authorities? A counselor?"

"Sort of," Julie replied, "but the thing is, it's my fault. Also, I can't prove that I didn't participate. I was drinking, and nobody forced me to. I passed out because of it. I shouldn't have been drinking. I haven't said anything because I didn't want to get into trouble and I didn't want to get Robert and his family into trouble either. I couldn't even bring myself to tell my mom for a long time, but I told her last week. She wants to kill whoever did it, but I wouldn't tell her who that was. I should, but I haven't. I was just hoping that, on some level, a deep, unrelenting guilt is eating him up inside. It makes me sick to watch him and his friends at school. He seems oblivious to the fact that he destroyed my life as long as he can continue with his. There's no way I could just move on like he has. Everyone knows that it's a picture of me. Nobody knows it's him."

Emily felt complete empathy for her. What an impossible situation she was dealing with. But she couldn't wrap her head around Warren's involvement.

Susan sighed heavily. "Julie, you need to stop beating yourself up over this. It is not your fault. You didn't ask for this no matter what you were doing at the time, and *nobody* has the right to post unauthorized, intimate pictures for the world to see without your permission. To post those pictures for their own amusement is beyond disgusting. It's immoral. And, Julie, I believe you 100 percent," Susan concluded.

"Me too," said Peter.

"It makes me sick to say this, but so do I," Emily replied. It was then that the tears came for her. She sat on the opposite side of Julie and put her head on her shoulder.

Susan approached her. "That's probably enough for tonight," she said, "but before you go, I just want to say a couple of things. First, I fully support you, and we are all here for you whenever you need us. Second, I want you to talk to someone. I don't mean me or Peter or Emily, although you can certainly keep doing that whenever you need to. It's obvious to me that this is, understandably, tearing you up inside. From what Emily's told me, you've come so far since the beginning of the year. But you seem to be placing blame on yourself where it shouldn't be. It may help to safely talk about everything that you're thinking and feeling—not only to make you feel better but also to help you see clearly how you should handle this situation moving forward. You were treated horribly, and that should have some consequences for whoever was involved. At the very least, he should have to own up to what he did.

"Oh…and third, I don't think you should drive home. You can leave your car here. I can give you a ride home if you want."

"It's OK, Ms. P, I can give her a ride," Peter said. "Her house is about five minutes from ours...well from mine...but from where yours will be again soon!"

Susan and Emily walked them to the door and watched Peter lead Julie to his car. She looked like a lifeless rag doll as he helped her in to the passenger's side.

Susan was concerned. "We need to check on her tomorrow, Em. After she gets a good night's sleep," she said.

Emily nodded, gave her mom a long hug, and dragged herself up the stairs to bed. Over and over in her head she wondered how she could be such a bad judge of character. There had been a lot of red flags, but she had always believed that Warren was one of the good guys. It would be hard to trust her gut again for a long time.

Before going to sleep, she picked up her phone and checked it for the first time since she'd left for the dance. She had a bunch of new messages, including twelve new texts from Warren. She put her phone down, laid her head on her pillow, and considered ignoring them or even deleting them, but she knew she would never get to sleep if she didn't read them. With a groan, she picked her phone back up and opened them.

"Can we talk?"

"Em, I meant what I said. I want to make this work."

"I know I have some things to work on, but I am going to do this."

"Emily, pls answer me."

"Where RU?"

The texts got more and more desperate from there. Emily stared up at the ceiling, contemplating how to respond. It took her about thirty seconds to decide that it was best to just rip the Band-Aid off. Maybe he would leave her alone after he found out that she knew. At this point, his relationship with Jake was the least of her worries. She texted back: *"Julie told us everything."*

She immediately saw bubbles pop up on her screen, but they disappeared. Warren was obviously taking his time deciding how to respond.

Fifteen minutes went by before she received his reply:

"Correction: Julie told you everything that she knows, but she didn't tell you everything."

That was *not* the reply Emily was anticipating, and she wasn't sure if Warren was going to try to make excuses for himself or if there was actually something more to the story. All she knew was that she had no reason to doubt Julie. She had watched her behavior since the

158

first day of school and had seen the way Julie's skin crawled at the mention of Warren's name. There was obviously a legitimate reason for that.

"Umm...not really sure what you mean by that, but I totally believe Julie. Nothing you could say would ever make me understand how you could do something like that. I thought I knew you. I couldn't have been more wrong."

Warren's reply came back.

"You should believe her. She is right about everything except who is responsible. I have done some things I am not very proud of since that night, but not ON that night."

Emily thought about the letter "J" on the hand in the picture. It was Warren's. That was all the proof that was needed.

"I know that it's your hand in the picture. Julie knows and I am sure you do too. You're just lucky she didn't take this to the police. I am way too tired to debate this over text. Don't text me again."

But he did, surprising her again and leaving her wrestling with a decision for the rest of her fitful night.

"Last one: Meet me tomorrow at Sawyer Park at 10 am by the entrance to the walking trail. There is more than one victim here. I will explain then if you give me a chance."

"Grrrrrrrrr!" Emily said through gritted teeth. She'd had enough drama for one night. She threw her phone to the floor and tried to go to sleep. It didn't come easily.

Chapter 18

The Other Side

Emily woke up at six the next morning. She estimated that she had gotten a total of fifteen minutes of sleep. It was Sunday, which meant no training. Technically, her coach forbade the team to run on Sundays, but Emily was desperate. She ached from exhaustion as she rolled out of bed, but she knew that once her feet started hitting the asphalt, she would be a much happier person. So she slipped on her sneakers, grabbed her earbuds, and headed out the door. The house was still quiet when she left.

She grappled with her decision for every minute of her run. Should she hear Warren out? Should she even believe what he had to say? Obviously, he had been hiding something all of this time, and he had lied to her when she asked him about it. But she kept going back to the fact that, deep down, she didn't think he was capable of hurting Julie for sport. Her gut told her that there probably was more to the story.

By the time she ran back down the driveway, she felt much more like herself. And her decision had been made: she would meet

Warren and at least listen. She did not believe he was evil or dangerous. If nothing else, she might be able to trust her instincts again.

Emily took a shower, changed, and grabbed some breakfast. By then, Jake and her mom had started stirring.

"Good morning, Em. I hope you got some sleep," Susan said as she was pouring some coffee. When she looked up, she noticed Emily carrying her dirty running clothes, which would eventually make their way to the laundry room on the other side of the kitchen. Susan stopped suddenly, deducing that Emily had not just rolled out of bed as was her norm on Sunday mornings. "Wait...you went for a run already? Aren't Sundays supposed to be your day off?" she asked.

"Coach gave us yesterday off for homecoming, so, technically, that was my rest day," Emily said as she took a bite of peanut-butter-and-banana toast. "And, yeah, I got a bit of sleep, but not much." Then she threw in, "Warren was texting."

Susan's eyebrows shot up immediately, and Emily clarified.

"At first, he was just texting for whatever, but I told him right away that Julie told us what happened. He said something about how she told us everything that she knows, but that she may not know everything. I don't know. It was pretty cryptic. Anyway, he wants to meet to tell me his side of the story. That's what kept me awake and kinda why I went running. I was trying to decide what I should do."

"And?" Susan said

"And, I think I want to know. Otherwise, I will always wonder. At best, it will help me understand how anyone could do that to another human being. At worst, I walk away and never talk to him, which is what I was going to do anyway.

"I'm meeting him at the park at ten. I'll call you right afterward so you know I'm safe. I've told you all along that my gut says he is a good guy. Totally imperfect, but not mean. I don't understand how I could be that wrong."

Susan looked hesitant. "Can you take somebody with you, Em? Just to be on the safe side?"

Emily responded with an exaggerated eye roll. "Mom, this is the very same person you have allowed me to be alone with dozens of times. Plus, I need the truth. I don't think he would be as open if I came with a chaperone."

"I suppose that's true," Susan responded. "Call me immediately when you get there and as soon as you're done."

Forty-five minutes later, Emily was sitting on the swings at the Sawyer Park playground when Warren arrived. He looked pale and uneasy in his gray UConn sweatpants and blue Brighton hoodie. He approached her cautiously and sat down on the swing next to her. He was quiet for a minute or two, but Emily let him take the lead.

Finally, Warren cleared his throat. "So, I want to start by apologizing because, although I didn't do anything wrong initially, I also didn't do anything right later on."

Emily laughed. She was half-amused and half-frustrated. "Warren, you have to stop speaking in this weird cryptic code, or I will never understand," she said.

Emily's laughter seemed to put Warren more at ease, and he continued. "I wasn't forthcoming with you, and I tried to sweep some stuff under the rug instead of supporting Julie. I was selfish. I was only concerned about my own reputation, but I didn't do what you think I did. I just don't know how to prove that to you or to anyone else. At first, I figured that if I just ignored the situation altogether, it would eventually blow over. When I saw how much it affected Julie, though, I knew I should have done more.

"But I'm a victim too, though nobody would understand that. And it's been eating me up inside for months."

"It's gonna be tough for me to understand your perspective unless you give me some details, Warren," Emily said stretching out her hand to his. He immediately held on. As each moment passed, she knew she was right about him. He was not dangerous. He was just crumpled and confused.

"Yeah, I know. I guess I should start at the beginning. This is the first time I've talked about it since it happened. It's just been easier to pretend it never happened at all. I'm not sure what Julie told you, but, as I said last night, it was probably the 100 percent truth. I'm not disputing what happened. She has every right to hate me, and it kills me because we actually hit it off really well that day."

Warren paused for a few moments, letting out a long sigh. "OK, so, here it goes. As you probably already know, we were hanging out together all day at Robert's beach house. We were just chilling, playing some games and drinking a little. We all grabbed pizza and built a bonfire just after the sun went down. We kept hanging out and, at some point, she and I passed out on a beach lounger next to the fire. It was totally innocent. I only woke up when she jumped out of the chair. I'm not sure what time it was, but it was pretty late and she was crying. Hard. I tried to ask her what was up, but she picked up her bag and booked it out of there as fast as she could. I was kinda worried about her, though, so I followed her, calling her name over and over and asking what was the matter. I chased her all the way to her car. As she was getting in, she looked me straight in the eye and screamed, 'I cannot believe you did this.' Then she just drove away. I'll never forget the look on her face as long as I live. That's the last time we spoke.

"At first, I thought she meant that I didn't wake her up or that I made her miss her curfew or something like that. But when I went back to the chair to get my things, I figured out what she was actually talking about. I picked up my phone and saw the photo on her feed. I saw that I had been tagged in it, and a lot of the other guys had too. A surprising number of them had liked it or even screen-shotted it and posted it to their own stories. It made me sick and honestly really sad. I mean, there was no doubt it was my hand. Everyone that was there would know that, and I'm not denying it. But I didn't take off her top. I definitely didn't take the picture or post it. I didn't know who did either, at least not right away. That's what I meant when I said there's more than one victim here. I get that Julie got the worst of the humiliation, and it was totally undeserved. She is really an awesome girl. It's just that I was embarrassed too and made to look like a total snake. That's not who I am. It was really bad for me. I just had no idea how to deal with the aftermath. I still don't. So I guess I just didn't deal with it, and I didn't help Julie deal with it either. That's where I was totally wrong."

"Damn," Emily muttered as she silently tried to process what Warren had shared so far. For the first time, she felt like he was being completely honest with her. "What happened next?" she asked.

"Well, I guess this is where it gets confusing for me. I assume someone thought that the whole thing was just a funny prank, so they staged it when we were both totally passed out." He paused to look Emily in the eyes and pleaded, "I really need you to believe me."

Then he continued, "I remember trying to figure out who would want to do that or who would be ignorant enough to consider it amusing. I went into the house and woke Robert up first. He hadn't seen it yet, but when I told him about it, he seemed genuinely disgusted. He was thinking much clearer than I was, and he suggested that we remove the tags and do our best to delete what we could. We did that right away. Honestly, though, the damage had already been done. We sent a group text to EJ and a couple of our other close friends who had been at the party. We wanted to know if anyone knew who was responsible. None of them had seen anything. We sent a second text to a several other guys who had been at the party. Some of them thought it was hysterical, a couple of them actually had the balls to congratulate me, but a bunch of them responded with 'not cool.' I couldn't even defend myself—all I could focus on was what people would think of me. I was so consumed by those thoughts that, at first, it didn't cross my mind that Julie was going through hell. I've been such an ass."

Warren started to sob. Any façade of confidence had completely dissolved. It was obvious that guilt had been crushing him and that hiding it for the past two months had taken its toll. Emily didn't think she could forgive him for abandoning Julie, but she was starting to see how it could have happened.

"Robert and I talked about a bunch of scenarios, but we decided not to say anything to our parents or to the police. I was afraid we'd get in trouble for drinking. I was even more paranoid about what would happen to my future if the police didn't believe me. There was no way I could prove that I hadn't willingly participated in this.

"From then on, I tried to ignore it, but in the back of my mind, I knew that Julie had good reason to believe that I did this to her. Every day since, I've spent waiting for the fallout, but it never came At least not from the direction I expected. I wrestled with my own guilt and anger but also from watching Julie struggle so blatantly. I was totally afraid to talk to her. I just stood back and let her suffer."

Warren let go of Emily's hand, stood up, and walked over to a giraffe-shaped bench next to the swing set. He sat down and placed his head in his hands. Emily couldn't tell if he was resting or crying. Either way, he was in serious pain.

She sat down next to him but didn't touch him. She wanted to give him some space, but she still had one question. "You said you didn't know right away who was responsible. Do you know now?" Emily asked

Emily could see Warren nod, his head still cradled in his palms. She didn't press further but gave him a few minutes of silence.

Warren finally raised his face. He stared straight ahead, looking out toward the soccer field as he spoke. "I just found out last night. While you were dancing with Jake, I was standing against the back wall with a couple of guys. They were all watching you, and a few of the guys were commenting on how awesome you looked. Paul Evans asked what the hell you were doing with a dork like me, and everybody laughed. But it was Kenny Turner's response that shocked me. He said that I had him to thank because he was responsible for making me look like a real 'player.'

"That seemed to come out of left field, until I remembered that he had been at the bonfire that night. He came at me for a fist bump with a big, goofy self-congratulatory grin on his face. I gave him a fist bump to the gut and walked back to the dance floor to find you. My mind was reeling, and you know the rest. You broke up with me a little while later, but it seemed too late and too overwhelming to begin to explain any of this last night."

Emily could tell that he was done—in every sense of the word. She didn't blame him. She was pretty spent too, and she had just been on the outskirts of this whole situation. She had to admit, she felt more empathy for Warren than she had anticipated. But that was all she felt. Hopefully, today's confession was the first step in a marathon of actions that would help him make things right. For himself and for Julie.

"Warren," Emily said, not wanting to burden him further, "I believe you. I've always known, deep down, that you have the potential to be one of the good guys. I'm not sure what any of the potential ramifications are for you or for Kenny, but I do know that Julie deserves better than what you've given her. She deserves an explanation and an apology. I honestly think that when you get your head sorted out, you should talk to her. It may seem too risky, but I think it could be cathartic. But before you even think about talking to

Julie, you need to talk to somebody who can help you straighten things out. How about we go to see Mr. Grant on Monday?"

"Yeah, I guess I can try that," Warren replied halfheartedly after a long pause. "I don't know how to start talking to Julie. The more time went by, the harder it became. I know I need help. Since you know the truth, from both sides, can you please just tell her that it wasn't me? You can share details or not, but can you please tell her that I did not do it and that I would never intentionally destroy her like this? Can you tell her how sorry I am for the way I've handled myself since that night?"

Warren was absolutely begging her for help. It broke Emily's heart to see him turn into a shell of the young man she thought she had known. She nodded slowly, considering her response carefully. "I'm going to ask my mom for help, but I promise to try to start the conversation with Julie if you promise to see Mr. Grant first thing on Monday."

"Deal," Warren said wearily. He gave Emily a weak hug. "Thanks for listening, Emily. Thanks for believing me. I guess I'll see you on Monday morning."

Emily sat on the giraffe bench and watched Warren shuffle his way back to his car. Before he got in, she shouted, "Shoot me a text when you get home!" She wanted to know he was safe.

He gave her a halfhearted thumbs-up before climbing into the driver's seat.

What a difference twenty-four hours can make, Emily thought as she watched him go.

Chapter 19

What Would Mom Do?

As promised, Emily texted her mom when she was done talking with Warren.

"*All good. Heading home. Can we talk when I get there, Mom?*"

Susan's response was rapid, which surprised Emily. Usually it took her mom three hours to respond to a text. She never had her phone with her. Today, Emily assumed, she had been anxiously waiting to hear from her.

"*Sure, baby. Are you OK?*" Susan replied

"*Yep. Coming home now. Talk to you then. Love you!*" Emily said.

When she got home, Susan was waiting for her on the steps. Emily was surprised to see Peter's car there. She also noticed that Julie's car was already gone. She ran up to her mom and gave her a big hug, holding on for as long as she could. She could hear the sounds of a guitar coming from inside the house and Jake's deep, shaky voice howling, "Booooooo me." She smiled, thinking how quickly he had learned that song.

Susan read her daughter's mind. "Peter dropped Julie off to get her car just before you texted. I asked him to stay so we could talk uninterrupted. I figured he could entertain your brother for a little while."

She took Emily by the hand and led her to the back patio. It was blissfully peaceful back there, even if it was a little chilly. It was Emily's favorite part of Aunt Bridget's house.

They took a seat at the round teak table. Susan had put a pot of tea out for them, knowing how the feeling of warm tea sliding down her throat always relaxed Emily.

Emily took her time filling her mother in on what Warren had told her. She tried to recall every detail of what he had said, except one. She added her own observations about his demeanor and complete transparency. Susan, for her part, did her best not to interrupt as her daughter spoke. She listened intently to every word. The only detail Emily left out was who Warren believed was responsible for the post. She wasn't sure it was her place to spread accusations just yet.

"Mom, I think we need to help them both," Emily concluded.

"Em, I think we need to find someone who is *qualified* to help them both," Susan replied. "I don't think either of us is that person, but we can definitely get the ball rolling. I'll tell you what, why don't you call Julie and see where her head is. If she feels like she's ready, we can share what you heard today. Either way, she should probably meet with Mr. Grant on Monday too. We can let him take it from there."

Emily agreed.

"Let me know what she says," Susan said as she gave Emily a quick kiss on the top of her head and went back inside. "If she ends up stopping by and you'd like some moral support, I'm here all day. You can find me in the laundry room."

Emily sent Julie a text: *"I know you are probably exhausted, but I found out a few things that you may want to know. If you want to talk, just text. I hope UR OK."*

Then she sat back, closed her eyes and finished her tea while she listened to the muffled sounds of Peter and Jake working in the background. Fifteen minutes later, she was startled by the buzzing of her phone. *"Is it OK if I come over now?"* Julie texted.

"That would be great. We'll be here all day," Emily responded.

Within half an hour, Julie was at their front door. She looked like she had just come out of the shower. Her hair was wet, and she was dressed in plaid pajama pants and a sweatshirt.

"I'm sorry if I got here too quickly," she said breathlessly, "but for two months now what happened, and all of the questions that go with it, have been rolling around in my head. Now that I told you, I feel like I need answers. When you texted, I almost couldn't wait to get here. Does that seem weird?"

"Not at all!" Emily laughed, leading Julie into the living room to sit down. "I don't understand how you held that in for so long."

When they were sitting down together, Julie turned to Emily and asked what she'd found out. Emily started cautiously, gently sharing what she'd learned from Warren that morning. Emily was careful not to take sides or to present opinions but just to give Julie the facts that she so desperately needed.

Julie surprised Emily with her response. "Thank you. Honestly, I'm not totally sure what to believe. On some level, I feel relieved. I felt like I had a connection with Warren that night. Maybe I shouldn't tell you that. I've struggled a lot trying to understand how he could turn so harshly on me, even if he didn't know me that well. It's a relief to even consider that he might not have been responsible. On the other hand, I feel even more vulnerable and exposed, because I really have no idea who would be cruel enough to victimize both of us."

Emily responded quickly. "Warren was just plain wrong not to share this with you in the first place. As time went by, he said it just got harder and harder for him to approach you. That was childish and immature. Part of the reason he didn't tell you was because he didn't know how to prove he wasn't responsible. Like you just said, he didn't know who was. Last night at the dance, he finally found out. I wasn't sure if you wanted to know or not. If you do, I'll tell you."

"Yes!" Julie said emphatically. "Wouldn't you?"

"I'm honestly not sure how I would feel in your shoes," said Emily. "You're the only one who knows."

At Julie's continued insistence, Emily shared the rest of the story. Julie absorbed it thoughtfully. "Who the hell is Kenny Turner?" Julie responded when she finally spoke.

"Just some jerk football player who's sort of friends with Robert," Emily said with unmasked sarcasm. "He always sits at the opposite end of our lunch table with Reed and EJ. He's that big dude with red hair and freckles. I think he's been hit in the head one too many times over the years—it's obviously impaired his judgment and made him slightly delusional. After he told Warren that he'd improved his reputation as a ladies' man, Warren was so pissed. Kenny went in for a fist bump, and Warren punched him in the stomach. Hard. I would have paid good money to see Kenny's reaction to that."

A slight smile appeared on Julie's lips, but she still seemed distracted. She obviously had more to consider now that she knew the whole story. Emily felt a weight lifted off her chest to not only understand what had happened but to have shared it with Julie. It wouldn't change what happened, but it might help Julie start to move on.

"Again, thanks Emily. Thanks for being honest and for sharing what Warren told you. I don't know if I'll ever be able to forgive him, but you've given me some food for thought. I have a lot to work out before that happens."

"I get that, Julie," Emily responded.

"Before I head home, can I say hello to Jake?" Julie asked.

"Sure, I know he would like that. He's with Peter in his room. I'll get them."

When Emily returned with Peter and Jake, the air around Julie still felt thick and heavy. Jake sensed it, for sure. When he saw Julie, he bent down and pushed the large coffee table aside, making extra room in front of the couch where she was sitting. Then, he extended his hand toward Julie and said, "Do do do do do do do da."

Emily smiled as she watched Julie consider what Jake was trying to say. She restrained herself from translating, wanting to see if Jake had made himself clear. Even if his words were lacking, his gestures and facial expressions almost always made up for it.

After a brief moment, a slow grin spread across Julie's face. "Yes, Jake, I *do* want to dance." she said, taking his hand and getting up to her feet to face him. Peter grabbed his guitar and played a medley of Zac Brown Band, the Dudes, and, of course, the Chicken Dance.

Chapter 20

The Sun Comes Up

Monday morning turned out to be a damp, drizzly, and slightly depressing late-October morning. As she and Jake drove through the fog toward school, Emily was anxious about what today would bring. She was especially worried about whether or not Warren would keep his promise to go and see Mr. Grant. On their drive in, Emily envisioned the morning in a dozen ways. Her biggest fear was that Warren would just paint on the "popular guy" mask and pretend the weekend had never happened.

Not one of the visions that ran through her head even came close to what actually happened.

When Emily pulled the Jeep into her usual parking spot, she was surprised to see Warren's car backed in beside her. She hadn't spoken with him since Saturday except to text him to let him know that she had shared his story with Julie and that Julie was taking her time trying to make sense of it.

"Don't get out yet," she said to Jake as she rolled down her car window. Warren did the same. "Ready for today?" she asked cautiously, still trying to feel out which Warren she might be dealing with.

"Ready as I'll ever be," he responded. Then he craned his neck around a bit to look further into her car. "Hey, Jake."

It was the first time Warren had ever directly acknowledged Jake's existence. Emily tried to hide her delight, though, because they had bigger issues to tackle today.

"Ha," Jake responded as he grabbed Emily's hand and brought it to his face. After years of speech therapy, Jake knew that if he wanted to learn to say a new word, he needed someone to help him figure out how to move his mouth in the right way.

"Excuse me a sec, Warren," Emily said. "He's actually trying to say hello back to you. He just doesn't know how to make his mouth say your name."

Emily had attended so many speech therapy sessions when she was younger that she knew how to cue Jake to make certain sounds. She used her fingers to form his lips into a "w," looked directly into his face, and said, "Warren." Sometimes, just showing Jake how to start a word would help him be able to say the whole thing. Jake made a couple of attempts before he came out with something that sounded like, "Wawa."

With Emily's help, Jake repeated the phrase all together. "Hi, Wawa."

"Wow!" Emily said. "Great job, Jake." She gave him their own high five, in which they bumped elbows instead of hands. Then, she turned to Warren, her eyes bright with excitement. "You have no idea what a big deal it is that he learned your name that quickly. That only happens when he is super motivated to learn a new word."

Before she finished the statement, Jake had unbuckled his seat belt and bolted out the door. He quickly ran around to Emily's side of the car and peeked in her open window. Warren looked surprised and slightly scared.

"Sah sah sah up," Jake said, excitedly jumping up and down and looking from Emily to Warren. They were both still in their cars, windows open, with Jake in the middle of them. Jake didn't even realize he was getting drenched in the rain.

Emily giggled and rolled her eyes thinking, *Here we go again*, but she no longer felt embarrassed or ashamed of what she had to do. She also cared much less about what Warren thought of her than she would have just a few days ago. She peered around her brother at Warren and explained, "Jake is communicating that he has something he wants to say to you. Ever since he was a toddler, words have come out easier if he sings them. The words might not mean what you think, but each song he requests conveys something specific. Oh, and get ready for a treat, because I'm going to be helping him out."

She looked at Jake and said, "Ready?"

Jake nodded emphatically as the raindrops formed on the tip of his nose. He couldn't have looked happier.

Emily started:

The sun comes up...to get your body moving
The sun comes up...to brighten up our days
The sun comes up...for everyone together
The sun comes up...so come on out and play

Jake turned toward Warren and sang his approximations for "sun" and "up" as Emily sang the rest of the words. They sang the whole thing twice through. When they stopped, Jake looked expectantly at Warren, as if he would automatically know what Jake was trying to say.

Warren's head tipped toward the sky. He looked perplexed. "Uhhhh, there's no sun out today, Jake," he stammered.

Jake stopped jumping and gave Emily a look that clearly said, *Is this guy for real?* Emily couldn't help but burst out laughing.

When she regained her composure, she apologized to Warren and tried to explain. "Jake learned that song when he was really little. When he was young, he would use it to ask kids if they wanted to play with him. Now, he uses it more to just say he wants to hang out with you. Like, maybe if you would just spend a minute or two walking with us to his classroom? Would that be OK?"

"Ya!" Jake said with a fist pump and turned back toward Warren.

"Sure, sounds good. I think I can handle that," Warren said.

As Warren got out of his car, Jake linked his arm tightly with Warren's and pulled him toward the door. As usual, Emily walked a short distance behind. She really wished she could see Warren's face right now. Instead, she spent a moment pondering why Jake suddenly wanted to be friends with Warren. It seemed odd that Jake wanted to spend time with him after Warren had treated him so badly at homecoming. Jake was a heartwarming combination of pure childishness and indefinable emotional wisdom. You definitely had to look far beyond the surface to truly know him.

As they opened the door to Jake's hallway, Emily finally realized why he had chosen today to "hang" with Warren: he somehow sensed that Warren needed a pep squad today, and that is exactly what he got the second they entered the school. Jake's entourage was ready and waiting for him, and they seemed to have doubled in number this morning. They surrounded him, and Warren, with a stronger-than-normal energy as they headed up the hallway. Even though Emily couldn't see his face, she could sense that Warren was smiling.

But the smile dissipated quickly when they reached the door to room 64.

"Damn!" Emily muttered to herself as she jogged forward to catch Jake and Warren. She was kicking herself for forgetting that Julie would be the first one to greet Jake when they got to his room. Instead of crouching in the corner, as she had for the first month of school, Julie now stood in the hallway outside the door. When Warren saw her there, he released himself from Jake's grip and froze in his tracks.

Jake was oblivious to the nonverbal communication between Julie and Warren, so he just continued happily on toward his classroom door with a quick hello and high five for Julie.

Once Jake was safely in his classroom, his entourage went on with their day, leaving Warren, Julie, and Emily standing awkwardly in the silence they left behind. After a few, long moments, Warren took two more steps forward so that he was face-to-face with Julie. She didn't make eye contact, but she didn't turn away.

Warren cleared his throat and, softly but earnestly, said, "Julie, I cannot tell you how sorry I am. I only hope you will let me explain myself to you someday." Though she kept her eyes downcast, his desperate gaze never left her face.

When he didn't get a response, he walked back toward Emily and said, "It's fine if you want to just go to class, I can find my way to Mr. Grant's on my own. Thanks for your support." He sounded resigned.

He headed down the hallway toward the office, and Emily watched him go. When he was out of sight, she turned back toward Julie. She was still leaning against the wall, eyes burning a hole into the linoleum floor. Emily put her arm around her and said, "Well, it's a start."

Julie nodded as she looked up at Emily and said, "Shoot me a text when he's done with Mr. Grant. I need to see him today too."

"OK. I will. That's probably a good idea," Emily said.

Julie met her gaze and said, "Definitely, and I will do my best to talk to Warren sometime soon."

"I honestly think that's all we can ask for at this point," Emily responded. "You are a much braver person than I would be in this situation. I hope you know that."

Chapter 21

Rehearsals

The next few weeks were ones of transition, from the activities of the early school year to those that would lead them into the midwinter chill. Emily was relieved that the pressure of cross-country was over for her and that her season had been a success. She had placed second in the state finals (by a thousandth of a second) and had two solid full-ride college offers to consider. Indoor track had started, but compared to the stress of the cross-country season, that would be a breeze. She was looking forward to some downtime to spend with her friends.

Jake had started drama rehearsals with Peter and Julie, and he seemed to be doing well. The temporary plan that they'd made with Susan looked like it might turn out to be a long term one. Along with his small parts, Peter had also gotten understudy to Nathan Hawkings, who had won the lead in every single school play ever since their *One Fish, Two Fish* show in kindergarten. Maybe she was biased, but Emily always thought that Peter's voice was warmer and much more powerful than Nathan's. She could listen to Peter's voice all day, and some days she felt as if she did. Julie, for her part, was finally getting involved in school activities, which was a great sign. She was working with the stage crew, so both she and Peter were able to hang out with Jake quite a bit during early rehearsals. Warren still retained enough of his old charm to get the male romantic lead, opposite Olivia Skyler.

Though they were no longer together as a couple, Emily was very happy for Warren. Since homecoming, he had been slowly but noticeably changing for the better. His overcompensating confidence seemed to be a thing of the past. In its place was a new humility and peace that Emily truly enjoyed. They spoke often, so Emily was aware that he continued to meet with Mr. Grant at least twice a week. Julie did as well.

Warren had mentioned feeling a deep relief following the first few meetings with Mr. Grant, mostly because he felt believed. Mr. Grant had assured him that he was not being accused of a crime. More importantly, he was helping Warren deal with the tremendous guilt that had been crushing him since the end of the summer.

Julie was understandably tight lipped about what she was working on with Mr. Grant, but Emily sensed a steady change in her, especially since she'd found out that Warren had not intentionally attacked her. To Emily's knowledge, Julie and Warren had still not spoken, but Julie was able to be in the same room as Warren without being overly anxious or appearing physically ill. It was progress.

In fact, Julie and Warren were sitting at the same lunch table most days, albeit at opposite ends. Actually, Emily, Warren, EJ, Robert, Nat, and Sophie all sat at Jake's lunch table now. It was getting pretty crowded, but it was better than the alternative, which was eating at their old table with Kenny every day. After what he had done to Julie and Warren, Emily lost her appetite at the mere thought of him.

Honestly, Emily enjoyed eating with Peter, Jake, Julie, and their friends. They were a laid-back, easygoing, and welcoming group. She and her friends had felt comfortable with their new setup immediately. One day, a few weeks after homecoming, three visiting students sat at the table at lunchtime, which forced some seats to be rearranged. On that day, Julie and Warren were only separated by Peter, who sat between the two. Emily quietly noted that neither of them moved to another table to avoid each other, and she smiled to herself. The tension between them was no longer even remotely palpable.

That day, Peter was talking about a new set that had been donated to the Brighton drama club. "Mrs. Sharrington said it was donated by something called the Sawyer Leigh Grant Memorial Fund.

She said it's the same fund that was used to build Sawyer Park," Peter explained.

"Hey, that's Mr. Grant's little sister!" Warren and Julie said in unison. Everyone just stared at them. They looked at each other and smiled, only slightly.

Emily broke the silence. "Really? Sawyer Park is named after Mr. Grant's sister? I honestly didn't know that!"

"Yup," Julie responded, "Mr. Grant had a sister who passed away when she was about eight years old. Her picture is hanging up on the wall in his office. I am really not sure exactly what happened to her. I know he mentioned that she had cerebral palsy."

"Oh! I saw her picture when I was in his office," Emily said. "I remember thinking how much the girl in the picture looked like Mr. Grant and his son. I even thought it might be his daughter."

To everyone's surprise, Warren joined the conversation. "Julie's right," he said. "Mr. Grant told me a little about his sister too. She had CP, and she and Mr. Grant's mom both died in a fire many years ago. They were staying at a hotel in California. Mr. Grant wasn't with them because he was in college at the time, but he said that his mom couldn't get Sawyer out in time. The memorial fund is from donations, but also from a settlement with the corporation that owned the hotel. I think he said that the smoke detectors at the hotel weren't working. By the time they realized that there was a fire, it was too late."

Julie took up the story. "Mr. Grant said that he and his dad never wanted the money, so they built the playscape at Sawyer Park to be accessible to all kids. They put the rest in a fund to give small grants to the community. It's so sad, though, what happened to her."

"It really is," Warren agreed. "I can't even imagine losing a sibling." Julie and Warren held eye contact for a fleeting second before he looked away and pushed back from the table. "And speaking of Mr. Grant, I have a meeting with him in five minutes. I'll see you at rehearsal."

The first few days of indoor track were kind of a joke. Not much running was happening, so it was more of a social hour than anything else. Emily knew the drill, and she had assumed that coach would let them go after only an hour or so. She had told Susan she would just take Jake home after rehearsal today to save her mom a trip.

Emily walked into the auditorium, expecting to see a chaotic scene. Rehearsals had really only just gotten under way and, though she had never been in a play herself, she assumed it took a long time to make one run like a well-oiled machine. What she saw when she entered the room did not disappoint. There was a good deal of commotion both on and around the stage area. Various small groups were gathered, running lines or learning songs.

She took a seat in the very back of the auditorium so she didn't disturb any of the activity and, truthfully, so she didn't distract Jake. Peter and Julie had hinted that Jake was working on his own part, but they wouldn't tell her what that was. To the right of the stage, on the floor in a far corner was Jake with Peter. It was a familiar sight, except that this time they had some company. Mrs. Kendelsworth, the speech and language therapist, sat in front of Jake as Peter played music from just over his right shoulder. Mrs. K, as most of the students called her, had some papers in front of her. They looked like a script or possibly some lyrics. She was using her hands to shape Jake's mouth into various positions, over and over again, helping him learn to say something. Emily's curiosity was piqued. Since so many of her friends were in the play, she had read some of the script. She had also seen most of the songs, which were much more complicated than the songs Jake knew. She wondered, with some concern, which song Jake could possibly learn in just a couple of months. It sometimes took him six months to learn a new word, and even if he could say it with help, that didn't mean he could *remember* how to say it on his own. That was the most frustrating part about his communication difficulties, in Emily's opinion. Even with Mrs. K's help, it seemed almost impossible that he would learn an entire song. Emily just didn't want him to be put in a position where he would be embarrassed.

As she chewed on that thought for a moment, her attention was drawn away from Jake to the back corner of the stage. In the shadows, it looked like there were two people running lines. On further inspection, Emily could see that it was actually Warren and Julie. They were sitting cross-legged in the corner. Since Julie was only part of the stage crew, Emily assumed that she didn't have any lines to run. It looked like they might be just having a conversation. Because they sat in partial darkness, Emily could not see the expressions on their faces. One thing that having a nonverbal sibling had taught her, though, was how to read body language. Julie and Warren's body language told her that they appeared to be having a relaxed and amicable discussion. It was a really unexpected sight, and it made Emily feel incredibly hopeful.

She couldn't wait to get the scoop.

Chapter 22

Without Words

"March 4…school play…Days Bright with Laughter…March 4…school play…Days Bright with Laughter…March 4…school play…Days Bright…with Laughter," Jake said endlessly from the day it was programmed on his talker until March 4 arrived. He could not have been more excited if he got to meet Santa Claus face-to-face.

It was driving everyone nuts. Each morning, it was the first thing Jake said. Each night, it was the last thing he said, and in between he said it at least fifty times a day. Susan had created a special Velcro calendar to help Jake understand how many more days he had to wait. At first it looked like an advent calendar on steroids. It had over ninety days on it, and it had taken her three entire days to make. But as the days dwindled from ninety-four to thirty to ten, it began to look much less overwhelming. As the days dwindled from ten to five to one, Jake's excitement rose exponentially.

Over those ninety-four days, a lot had changed for Julie and Warren. By the winter break, Emily would say they were actually friends. It hadn't been easy, and she had been witness to at least a dozen heated conversations between the two, along with many more deep and meaningful discussions. By late November, she felt as though they had truly worked through their issues and had grown to understand one another. Once they were on good terms, Mr. Grant had worked with them, together, to help them decide what to do about Kenny. In early December, there had been a formal meeting with the vice principal, Julie, Warren, Kenny, Mr. Grant, and their families. No criminal charges were brought against Kenny, but he was asked to do fifty hours of community service cleaning up the parks in town, including Sawyer Park. Emily was pretty sure that Mr. Grant had also worked with Kenny to help him at least acknowledge that what he'd done was wrong. At some point in mid-December, Kenny, of his own volition, created an Instagram post publicly apologizing to Warren and Julie for the "wrongs he had done" without specifically rehashing the incident. Emily had to admit that Mr. Grant was a pretty incredible resource.

After that, things had settled down nicely. The second half of their senior year was turning out to be much more peaceful than the first had been. Emily picked Jake up at rehearsals a handful of times. Each time, she saw the same thing: Peter working with Jake. Sometimes Mrs. K was there, and sometimes she wasn't, but Peter and

Jake always worked together. Peter was uncharacteristically tight lipped about what they were working on, though. Emily had talked to him about it on two occasions. She only wanted to know which song Jake was learning so she could see for herself what the words were and if they were within his repertoire. Both times, Peter had softly asked her just to trust him and promised that he would never do anything that would potentially embarrass Jake. It was killing Emily not to be in the loop, but she did feel incredibly reassured by Peter's responses.

On the morning of March 4, Jake could no longer contain himself. "Showtime, showtime, showtime, showtime, showtime!" he said. Thank goodness Mrs. K had not programmed that onto his talker until yesterday. Ninety-four days of that would have been a little too much to take. Emily was also thankful that today was a Friday, which meant it was a school day. Jake could drive his teachers crazy for a solid seven hours before Emily would have to hear "showtime" again.

Peter and Julie picked Jake up to bring him to the auditorium at about five thirty that afternoon. Jake ran to the car without even looking back or saying good-bye to Susan or Emily. Susan had to chase him down to give him his clothes. Jake would be changing before going on stage, but for now he was wearing his bright orange Big Bird shirt and favorite gray sweatpants. That would keep him comfortable while he waited for his big entrance.

Emily, Susan, and Aunt Bridget left a short time later to meet Patrick. The four of them filtered in early to grab a seat toward the front. Because he was well over six feet tall, Patrick always liked to have an outside aisle seat. They sat in the fourth row back toward the right side of the stage, with Patrick on the outside next to Emily, Susan, and Aunt Bridget. While they waited, Emily flipped through the program, trying to see which part Jake had gotten. She didn't see him listed in the cast, but on the bottom of the list of cast members she saw his name under "Special guest appearance." She continued to scan the program to find enough information to satisfy her curiosity. Finally, she saw that there would be a musical performance by Jake Prescott, Peter McKinley, Julie Wallace, and friends during the intermission.

Emily felt so anxious that she could hardly focus on the first act. The play itself was a beautiful musical story about four friends who'd grown up in a small town and where life had led them. The music was amazing. Nathan did well in his role, as did Olivia and Warren. Peter made three quick appearances in the first act, including one short solo performance that brought tears to Emily's eyes. Every once in a while, Jake would peek his head ever-so-slightly out of the side of the curtain and wave to his family. The last time he did, he had changed into his homecoming suit. He looked so handsome.

As the first act finished and the cast cleared away, Mrs. Sharrington walked to the center of the stage to make an announcement. "That was a wonderful first act, don't you think?" she said in her deep southern accent. The auditorium erupted in applause. As it faded away, she continued, "During intermission, we have a special treat for you. So go ahead and stretch your legs. As you do, three of our talented students will be setting up to bring you a performance you will not soon forget. Peter McKinley and Julie Wallace have written and composed an original song that will be performed along with Jake Prescott. Please look for the lyrics on the blue paper at the back of your program. The song is titled "Without Words.""

Finally, the mystery was revealed! How had Emily missed the blue paper when she had scanned the program? She immediately dug through the program and pulled the paper out as quickly as she could. She couldn't take her eyes off of it. The lyrics were breathtaking. They captured Jake's character in just a few words. But they were difficult and deep and completely beyond Jake's capabilities, which made Emily panic. She glanced wild eyed at her mother, who calmly looked at Jake with a huge smile on her face. Emily followed her mother's gaze to the stage and locked eyes with Peter. He must have seen the look on her face because he silently mouthed, "Trust me," to her. She exhaled the breath she had been holding, told herself to relax, and focused on the scene in front of her.

Jake was standing in the center of the stage, looking surprisingly settled to be in the spotlight. Julie stood just behind his left shoulder, and Peter sat on a tall stool just behind him on the right, holding his guitar. As the lights of the stage brightened slightly, Emily could see that there were about twelve other students forming two lines behind them. In front of the stage, out of sight and kneeling on the floor, was Mrs. K.

Peter strummed the first chord, and the background singers began to hum. They, along with Peter and Julie, slowly sang the words of the first verse, becoming quieter, on occasion, in order to allow Jake to sing the words that he had practiced. He also signed many more words, checking in with Mrs. K every once in a while for reassurance. The tempo of the song picked up when the chorus started, so Peter, Julie, and the background singers sang louder and faster as Jake signed. Emily was struck by the amount of practice and choreography it must have taken for everyone to learn how to sing this song with Jake. She choked up again.

At the beginning of the second verse, a sudden movement from her dad took Emily's attention off the performance. Patrick jumped up from his seat and took several large strides toward the stairs at the side of the stage.

An instant later, just as Patrick had almost reached the stairs, Emily saw what he had seen. There was a slit in the curtain, where it had not quite been shut against frame of the stage. In the small opening there was a figure, in an orange T-shirt, jumping and flapping his hands. At first, Emily could only see his back, but when he jumped around, Emily saw his face clearly. It was Nathan Hawkings, wearing Jake's Big Bird shirt. He was flapping in circles, with his tongue out and his eyes crossed. Two of his friends stood laughing as they watched. It was a blatant and horrific imitation of her brother, but it was obvious that Nathan had not intended the display to be visible to the entire audience.

Once Emily's brain registered what was happening, she followed her father backstage, unsure of what he might do or say. She climbed the stairs a second or two behind him.

Patrick cleared his throat loudly to get Nathan's attention. "Young man, kindly remove my son's shirt," he said with obvious restraint. "This display is very disappointing. You may have undeniable talent, but your character is sorely lacking."

"I totally agree, Mr. Prescott," came Warren's voice from the other direction. "Nathan, what you just did was not cool at all."

Nathan was caught completely off guard by the unexpected witnesses. His face was as white as a ghost as he looked from Warren to Patrick and back, not knowing who to address or what to say. "Sh-sh-sure thing, Mr. Prescott," he stammered as he quickly took the shirt off and tossed it on the ground. He tried to walk away from the uncomfortable situation, but his exit was interrupted by Mrs. Sharrington, who took him gently by the elbow and led him deeper backstage.

Patrick looked at Warren and said, "Thanks for the backup, son."

"No problem, Mr. Prescott. Jake deserves better than that," Warren replied.

"Come on, Dad," Emily said, "let's see if we can catch the end of the song."

As they returned to their seats, Emily was disappointed to see that the song had just finished. Nathan, who was so often in the spotlight, had stolen Jake's one shining moment out of pure ignorance. It completely infuriated Emily. The only saving grace was that Jake was oblivious to what had just happened.

Jake waved and smiled broadly as he left the stage. The crowd was giving them a standing ovation which, in an odd way, angered Emily even more. They had been able to witness what she had not. She choked back a sob, and Patrick put his arm around her and gave her a quick kiss on the side of the head. "It's all right, Em. Let's not let that idiot ruin our night, OK? I'm sure somebody got the whole thing on video. We can watch it with Jake later," he said.

Emily nodded as the rest of the group walked off stage. Mrs. Sharrington pulled Peter aside and whispered something to him. Peter looked surprised, but he nodded and hurried away. Mrs. Sharrington then took the microphone. "There will be a slight change in the cast for the second half. Unfortunately, Nathan Hawkings will be unable to continue in the role of William Kayden. Peter McKinley will be performing in his place."

"Yes!" Emily whispered under her breath. "That's what we call karma biting you in the butt, Nathan!" Her mom and dad both looked at her and smiled. They all knew for certain that they were in for a treat.

Peter killed it! Emily sat enthralled as she watched the second act. At the conclusion of the play, the audience rose to their feet again. They didn't sit down until well after the final bows were taken. As Peter, Olivia, and Warren ran off the stage for the last time, the crowd remained on their feet and began chanting. Initially, Emily thought they were cheering for Warren by name. After a moment or two, what they were saying became clearer to her, and she joined in fervently.

"Without Words! Without Words! Without Words!" the audience cried.

They were demanding an encore performance!

Emily was overwhelmed by the chant. She watched as Jake, Julie, Peter, and the background singers filled the stage again. This time, she took in the entire performance with tear-filled eyes and a grateful heart.

Without Words

An original song
Lyrics: Julie Wallace
Music: Peter McKinley
Performed by: Jake Prescott (and friends)

Verse 1:
I'm not lost
Though I may be sometimes silent

I'm not sad
Though my voice may not flow free

I'm not less
When my words are undiscovered
I'm not more
I am just as I should be

I am joy
I have endless perfect moments
I can smile
I can dance and I can play

I can dream
For a million different reasons
I can speak
In a thousand different ways

Chorus

Listen with your eyes
Listen with your mind
Listen to the hand that you are holding

Listen to my smile
Listen to my laugh
Listen to the things that I hold true

Listen with your heart
Listen with delight
Listen to the spirit deep within me
I will share with you the greatness of my story
…without words

Verse 2:
I can share
All the things that make me happy
I can hurt
When I carry too much weight

Just like you
I need love and true acceptance

Understand
You can help me find my way

Take your time
Stop and see the world through my eyes
I am love
I have purpose, I have strength

Walk with me
Through a million magic moments
Fill your heart
Watching wonder light my face

Chorus

Listen with your eyes
Listen with your mind
Listen to the hand that you are holding

Listen to my smile
Listen to my laugh
Listen to the things that I hold true

Listen with your heart
Listen with delight
Listen to the spirit deep within me
I will share with you the greatness of my story
…without words

Yes, I will share with you the greatness of my story, without words

Chapter 23

Happy Birthday

Emily sat on a metal chair at the long table in front of her. A feeling of peaceful contentment settled sweetly in her gut. The future, at least the very near future, looked promising and in control, in stark contrast to the roller coaster that had carried her through the past several months. Almost everything seemed to be settling down around her. She only wished that she, Jake, and her mom could be back at their house to enjoy it. Unfortunately, the fierce winter storms had arrived at the same time the insurance money had, so construction had not been an option for some time. Now, in late March, they were finally planning on breaking ground on the new and improved Prescott residence. That meant that they would be spending the summer at Aunt Bridget's house instead of back in their own. It was a beautiful house, and Aunt Bridget was gracious and welcoming, but something deep inside Emily just wanted to be home.

Nonetheless, Emily was happy that her own big decisions had been made and were just about to become official. It certainly seemed like an appropriate time to coast a bit before attacking the new challenges that awaited her after high school. Thankfully, she had been accepted into both of her top-choice colleges. She had decided to go to Providence to study psychology and, of course, run cross-country. Providence was only a ninety-minute drive from Brighton.

"Mimi!" Jake shouted, shaking Emily from her momentary introspection. Mrs. Anderson had taken him from PE class and escorted him into the small conference room at the last possible moment. Patrick ushered him around the table and told him to have a seat beside him. On her other side, Emily became aware that her mom was tightly gripping her hand under the table. Emily smiled at Jake and gave her mom's hand a squeeze before releasing it. Surrounded by her family, it was time.

Mr. Johnson, the athletic director at Brighton, made a brief statement. "Today, I have the pleasure of introducing an athlete who truly needs no introduction. She is both a talent and a treasure to this high school and the entire community. Emily Prescott has demonstrated character throughout her years at BRHS. She has proven herself academically, personally, and, without a doubt, athletically. She has broken records, captained our team, and kept her head held high through tragic events. She is an excellent student with a very bright future in front of her. That future, beyond these small walls, will begin in the fall at Providence College. I personally am looking forward to seeing what records she can smash when she gets there. We will continue to watch you, support you, and cheer you on with all of our might, Emily! Congratulations!" he said as he placed the letter of intent in front of her.

With her parents flanking her and about a dozen close friends and teammates gathered in the room in front of them, Emily signed the letter and committed to run cross-country at Providence. When she placed the pen back down on the table, she looked up into the small crowd. Some of them were clapping, and others were taking pictures on their phones. She gave her mom, her dad, and her brother a hug before the photographers from the school and local papers asked her to pose with her family for an official photo.

When they were done, the whole room applauded one more time. Emily blushed and mouthed, "Thank you," to everyone. She had never been comfortable being in the spotlight.

"Happy birthday," she heard.

Jake had left his seat and crept up behind Emily. "Happy birthday," Jake said through his talker.

"Jake, buddy, it's not my birthday," Emily said patiently.

Jake had no way of understanding what was happening right now. He knew it was a celebration, and he also knew Emily was the guest of honor. To Jake, all celebrations, with the possible exception of Christmas, were birthdays. After thinking about it for a second, Emily could see why he had chosen to say that. She put her arm around Jake and gave him a kiss on the cheek. "Thank you, Jake."

Jake smiled and grabbed his talker again so he could replay the message. "Happy birthday, happy birthday," he said again with the talker. "Bada, bada, BADA!" Jake said gleefully. Susan heard him and came over to stand beside him. She tried, unsuccessfully, to pull him from Emily's arm.

"Not now, Jake," Susan whispered. "We can sing and have cake when we get home. Does that sound OK?"

To that, Jake responded, "BADAAAAAAAAAAAAAY! Mimi!"

"It's fine, Mom," Emily said. She genuinely meant it.

"But, sweetie, today is about you," Susan responded.

"Yes, I know, Mom, but I think Jake knows too," Emily said, thinking that even just a year ago, this small situation would have made her angry. When she was younger, she'd felt as though Jake's constant singing stemmed from an inherent need to always be the center of attention. Recently, she had come to realize that that wasn't the case at all. In this moment, and in his own way, he was turning his attention where everyone else's already was. He was trying to congratulate his sister. He just didn't know the word.

"Are you sure, Emily? We don't always have to give in to his demands, you know," Susan was saying.

"Mom, he's fine! It's not a selfish demand. I honestly think it's more of a selfless request. I don't see any harm in obliging him this time," Emily said. She turned her head to face Jake. "Let's go, buddy. One...two...three..."

She, Jake, Susan, and Patrick placed their arms around each other and began to sing "Happy Birthday." A handful of the people that had gathered looked confused, but those who truly understood Jake's inner workings, including Warren, Peter, and Julie, approached the table, and joined in. It was undoubtedly a happy day, even if it wasn't a birthday.

When they got home, Emily picked up her phone to check it. Over the past three weeks, ever since the play, Emily had gotten back into the habit of checking social media every once in a while. Mostly, it was because a video of the "Without Words" encore had gone viral, and Emily couldn't get enough of watching its success grow every day.

Today, in addition to checking its progress, Emily noticed that there were two different stories about her signing. Since several of her friends had signed their letters of intent in the past month or two, Emily knew what to expect. Usually, it was a picture of the student and their family at the table, and a picture of the student signing. Along with the pictures, there was usually a small article about the student's past accomplishments and future plans. It was all pretty standard.

Both of the articles covering her signing, however, had chosen to accompany the story with a photo of Emily signing and a picture of her family singing "Happy Birthday." As Emily looked at the photos, she laughed and thought that *nothing* about being a Prescott sibling could ever be described as standard.

Chapter 24

Us

In early April, Emily became a little worried about Julie. She hadn't gone so far as to start wearing the hat again, thank goodness. But every morning for two weeks straight, she sat crouched in the corner by room 64, scribbling like crazy into a notebook. She still ate lunch and socialized each day at school. She still came over on the weekends to visit with Jake and hang out. And yet Emily was afraid history might be repeating itself.

Julie had become a great friend, but she often kept a lot to herself. Emily knew that she would talk only when and if she was ready. But Emily was not the only person who had noticed the change. Warren and Peter had seen it too. Ironically, Emily kept looking to Jake, and his sixth-sense superpower, to be the emotional thermometer when it came to Julie. She figured that if Jake's behavior toward Julie changed in any way, then it was time for them to truly worry. Emily watched him intently each morning, but he continued to greet Julie with a fist bump or high five, a quick conversation, and a song. It was the same routine they'd had for most of the year. Based on Jake's interactions, Emily concluded, there was absolutely no cause for alarm.

Unfortunately, Emily had a strong tendency to overthink things. So when Warren approached her and Peter with a promposal plan for Julie, it was just the distraction she needed. Given Warren's recent history with dance invitations, Emily really didn't expect much. To her great surprise, the sweet simplicity of his clever idea blew her away. The three of them spent just a few minutes going over it to see if it would work. When they decided that it would, they made a plan to meet at Jake's entrance the next morning to make it happen.

In the morning, the three of them walked in behind Jake and his posse. Honestly, at this point in the school year, Jake didn't need Emily to escort him to his room anymore. He hadn't for some time, but she had grown to enjoy being a witness to this every day. As the school year was winding down, she was keenly aware that there were not that many more opportunities for her to participate in this or any school ritual with Jake. She tried to burn the moments into her memory so she would never forget the impact her nonverbal brother often had just by being himself.

When they reached the door to room 64, Julie sat, as expected, crouched in a corner. She and Jake exchanged greetings and sang the good morning song before he walked through the door to the classroom. When he had disappeared, Julie briefly greeted the other three and went back to working in her notebook.

She was so intently focused on what she was doing that she didn't notice the sign that Warren was holding. Peter cleared his throat twice, but Julie remained in her own world. "Earth to Julie," Warren finally said. He held a small poster board that simply said "PROM?"

When she finally looked up and saw the sign, the plan went into action. Peter, Warren, and Emily started singing a familiar tune, with a few minor tweaks.

> *Put your hand out ONE*
> *Put your hand out TWO*
> *Come to prom with us*
> *And we'll go to prom with you*

Julie's eyes glistened with amusement. "How tender," she responded through her laughter. This time, the statement held affection rather than the bitter sarcasm that it held the first time she'd said it to Emily and Jake.

"Of course I will go to prom...with all of you," she said hesitantly. It sounded more like a question than an answer, possibly because only Warren held the sign.

"We thought a group date would be fun this time!" Peter responded.

Emily might have been overthinking things again, but she thought she saw the slightest look of disappointment flicker in Julie's eyes. She recovered quickly, though. "I couldn't agree more! I can't think of three people I'd rather spend prom night with. Let's go for it!" she said enthusiastically before sinking back down, almost immediately, to write again.

Peter and Warren headed off to get rid of the prom sign before their first class. Emily stuck around. She just couldn't take it anymore. "What gives, Julie?" she asked.

"Nothing, Em. Everything's fine! That was the world's best promposal ever! I just have to finish this today," Julie responded.

"You're honestly making me nervous, Jules. Every day for the past two weeks, you've been crouched in this corner again. I can't stand it. It feels like the beginning of the year all over again, except no hat and no caustic attitude," Emily finally admitted.

"Did anyone ever tell you that you need to lighten up, Em?" Julie laughed. "This time, I'm not here because I'm pissed off and depressed. I'm here because this is where I find my best inspiration."

"Inspiration?" Emily responded. "I'm not exactly sure what you mean by that, and it doesn't make me feel any better. I don't want to lose the Julie that I know now. None of us do."

Julie softened a bit and put her arm around Emily. "Em, you're not gonna lose me. I promise! We've both come way too far this year to turn back now. It's really not a big deal, but if you insist on knowing why I'm here, I'll just show you. When I do, you have to promise to leave me alone and let me get back to work. And please, keep it to yourself until I know for sure."

When Emily read what Julie handed her, she finally understood.

Chapter 25

Jake Quotient

The last few weeks of school passed by in frenzy for Emily and the rest of the senior class. Some parts of it were dreamlike, some were an absolute blast, and some were unavoidably bittersweet. As she sat back in her chair and waited for the remaining students to receive their diplomas, she couldn't help but reflect back on the year. From the nightmare of the late summer and first weeks of school through homecoming, the play, the prom, and every single ordinary day in between, it had been an adventure. Actually, it had been so much more than an adventure. In retrospect, this year had been a series of tiny gifts, and tonight, Julie's speech would be the ribbon that pulled all of those little moments together into one big, beautiful package of memories made and lessons learned. On that day, in the hallway, Emily had read the speech for herself. She couldn't wait to hear it spoken straight from Julie's lips.

After the final diploma had been received, Ms. Washington, the principal, stood at the podium. "As you know," she began, "this year we have chosen to close the graduation ceremony in a nontraditional manner. Rather than finishing with the principal's address, we have chosen to close with a speech from one of your fellow students. For the first time, we put out an open call to determine who would be chosen to speak in these precious, final moments before you go your separate ways. The subject for the speech was open ended, and the beauty of the contest was in the variety of topics that were addressed and the diversity of students who entered. The speech that was ultimately chosen was written by Miss Julie Wallace and is titled 'Jake Quotient.' Please welcome Miss Wallace to the stage. When she is done speaking, she will join Austin Belfast, our valedictorian, to lead the exit procession out of the auditorium. Once again, congratulations to everyone!"

Julie approached the stage confidently and took her place at the podium as the room fell silent.

"Thank you, Ms. Washington, for the kind introduction and for the opportunity to speak to the graduating class," Julie began. And then, she spoke some of the most beautiful words that Emily had ever heard:

"So, here we are. High school is done, and we are ready to move on. Does that mean we have learned everything there is to learn? Are you proud of all you've accomplished, of the awards

you've earned, of your GPA, of your class office, of your SAT scores, of your athletic stats, or of your future plans? Was high school everything that you expected it to be?

"For me, personally, it was not at all what I expected. What I learned throughout the course of this year was completely unplanned and unprecedented. It was not part of the curriculum or the extracurricular activities. Sometimes, the most important lessons are those that could never have been anticipated.

"When I returned to Brighton this year, after an eleven-year absence, I expected to pick up right where I'd left off. I expected to make friends easily and immediately. I expected to earn at least a 1200 on my SATs, to play varsity basketball, and to attend a good party or two. I expected a pretty normal senior year.

"What I did not expect is that I would have a best friend with Down syndrome. What I did not expect was that I would grow more and learn better than I ever have in my life because of my best friend. I did not expect to be standing here tonight, trying to inspire you with words that cannot possibly do justice to the admiration and gratitude I feel in my heart.

"I am, honestly, constantly amazed by the way my best friend deals with challenges and inspired by his many unique abilities. But

the thing I never expected to admire, and the thing I now aspire to achieve in my own life, is his level of inability.

"I think we could all benefit from having some of Jake's incredible inabilities. Though there are many, I will limit my list to the ones I admire most.

"First, Jake has the inability to deceive. He is pure and innocent. He cannot manipulate the truth either with little white lies or by giant premeditated manipulations. Without words, he tells you what he needs and how he feels, what he does and does not like. He has no reason to be anything but real. You never have to question his motivation or his loyalty because you know he is always true.

"Second, Jake has the inability to conform. He is not motivated to be like everyone else. He is motivated to be only exactly who he is. He does not wake up in the morning and wonder if anyone else will be wearing the same Elmo shirt or even if Elmo shirts are in style. Rather, he puts on the Elmo shirt because it makes him feel good. He has a unique understanding about what brings him joy. He isn't driven by the approval of others. He seeks happiness from within.

"Third, Jake has the inability to live to feed his ego. He has no desire to be the best or most popular. He does not manipulate the

truth to make himself look different or better than he is. Jake does not care about the number of 'likes' or 'shares' he receives, and he will never need to look to others to know his own self-worth. He accepts others, and he knows who makes him feel comfortable and who is comfortable with him. He would never think to put someone else down just to build himself up.

"Fourth, he has the inability to hold grudges. Jake has an incredible affinity for forgiveness. He readily sees the good in others, even when he has been wronged. Yes, he feels anger and disappointment sometimes, but he also quickly and innocently lets go of the hurt. He does not allow pain to weigh him down because it interferes with the joy in his heart.

"Fifth, Jake has the complete inability to cast judgment, to hate, or to discriminate. Jake doesn't care if you are popular or unpopular, rich or poor, average or beautiful, black or white. He doesn't care about your past mistakes, your future plans, or your reputation. He doesn't even notice these distinctions because they hold no importance to him. He doesn't see others through the tainted lens of preconceived notions, expectations, or jealousy. Instead, he sees others with total clarity. If he feels a connection with you, he will

want to spend time with you. Those who are loved by him are the recipients of a rare, pure, and unblemished love.

"Finally, when something or someone is important to him, he has the absolute inability to give up. Jake persists where most of us would walk away. When Jake first saw me, I was in a dark and very unfortunate place. Many of you know why. For weeks before our first meeting, I had been seriously contemplating suicide. On the day he first approached me, I sat in a corner, my journal in my lap, writing down the pros and cons of killing myself: the reasons I should continue to live and the reasons I seriously wanted to die. Jake had no way of knowing that. The first dozen or more times he tried to speak with me, I told him to get lost. But he sensed something in me, and I will never understand what that was. I will never understand how he knew or why he persisted. I often ask myself how long it would have taken for me to give up if I were in Jake's shoes. But Jake possesses gifts that are beyond my comprehension. It is not an exaggeration to say that this, by far, is the inability that I cherish above all others, because it is the one that literally saved my life.

"These are just six of the infinite inabilities that Jake possesses. Ultimately, they are indicative of the fact that Jake is not motivated by the things that seem so important to the rest of us as we

go through high school. He is only motivated by what he feels is right. As a result, his heart is pure, and he can only be true to himself and to those who are fortunate enough to be welcomed into his world.

"As you go through life, ask yourself if you might be a better person for living just a little more like Jake. Don't judge yourself solely by your salary, your achievements, and your possessions. Don't always aspire to find ways to prove your superiority. Don't compare your intelligence with others or look down on those who are not considered as smart or as accomplished.

"Rather, set aside your ego, your judgment, and your constant need for approval and, from this day forward, seek to improve your 'Jake Quotient.' Work toward acquiring a greater number of inabilities. Continue to strive to learn more, to better yourself, and to grow in important ways. But beyond that, always make sure that you never sacrifice your genuine self in order to move forward. Choose to follow the path that will allow you to remain exactly who you—alone—are meant to be. On this path, your inabilities will prove to be as invaluable as they are immeasurable because they will be indications of the trueness of your character.

"Right now, many of us are questioning what exactly the future holds for us. At this moment, every single one of us is full of

endless potential. Some of our future successes will be more visible than others. Whether seen or unseen, true successes can only be achieved if, as a result, we are personally fulfilled by them. Today, I stand here to offer you a single suggestion designed to push you toward your ultimate happiness, and that is this: From now on, take a little time each day to consider your inabilities and to measure your success not only by the impressiveness of your IQ but by an ever-increasing awareness of your JQ. At the very least, changing your perspective will change your life. At best, it may save someone else's."

With that, Julie walked down the stairs and off the stage, joining Austin and leading the procession of students out of the building. Emily could clearly see tears quietly streaming down Julie's face. As the students slowly filtered out into the fading sunlight, Emily began to scan the crowd for her. When she finally spotted her, she tried to make her way through the sea of students and family members to express her overwhelming pride and gratitude. Well before she could make her way over to Julie, however, Warren found her. Emily watched with a smile as he wiped her tears and wrapped her in a long, tender, congratulatory embrace.

Chapter 26

Celebration

Patrick closed McNalley's for a "private event," as the sign on the outside of the restaurant indicated. Emily's friends and their families had all been invited for a postgraduation celebration, catered by the restaurant. Patrick had hired a DJ and cleared some tables out to create a dance floor. Emily, Robert, EJ, Nat, Sophie, Julie, Warren, Peter, and Jake had the best time dancing, singing, and eating their fill of nachos.

At one point, during a much-needed rest, they all sat at the large corner booth, talking about future plans. Nat and Sophie had decided to go to UConn and room together. Both had gotten scholarships to play soccer. Robert was going to Cornell, and EJ was poised to enlist in the Navy. Julie had decided to study journalism at the University of Hartford. Going to a more local program would allow her to live at home to keep her mom company for now. She said that she wasn't quite ready to leave her mom alone. Warren would be a couple of hours away at NYU. He was leaning toward majoring in economics, with a possible minor in theater studies.

Patrick approached the group as they sat and talked. "Mind if I join you guys?" he asked.

"There's plenty of room for you, Mr. P!" Peter responded as he slid over to make room in the booth.

Patrick shook his hand and congratulated him. He handed Peter an envelope and said, "We cannot thank you enough for your hard work and friendship. We will never forget what you've done for Jake." Then, he quickly changed the subject to a less emotional one. He could only stand to speak about anything emotional for very brief periods of time. "So, what's up for you in the fall? What does the future hold for the famous Peter McKinley?" Patrick was referring to the notoriety that Peter had gained after the "Without Words" YouTube video went viral.

"Business, with a minor in music education. In my spare time, I'll take a few extra classes in special education and psychology. I'm hoping to do something with music therapy down the road."

"Son, I couldn't think of a career more suited to you," Patrick said with pride, and then he addressed the rest of the crew. "Now, who's ready for a good cry?"

Everyone looked up at Patrick at once. "Emily's mom coordinated a real tearjerker of a slide show. She's spent the last year taking pictures and collecting some from all of your parents," Patrick explained. He pointed to all of the kids as he spoke. "Come to the party room in five or ten minutes. Oh, and bring some tissues."

Emily gave it three minutes before she walked over to the party room off of the main dining area. She stopped short before she passed through the doorway, unnoticed by her parents, who were the only people in the room. She arrived just in time to see her dad handing her mom a gift. "What's this for?" Susan asked him. "I'm not the one that graduated today."

"Maybe not, but you are the reason she did," Patrick replied. "Open it before everyone comes!"

Susan quickly opened the package and gasped. It was a new digital camera, with three specialty lenses. "Patrick! I've missed mine so much this year!"

Susan had always loved photography, but her equipment had been destroyed in the fire. She had made do with taking pictures on her phone for the entire year, but the quality was nowhere near what she got from her camera.

"I know," Patrick replied. "I also know that you would spend every last dime of the insurance money on the kids or put it in savings before you would ever buy anything for yourself. You've worked so hard to create a safe and stable life for our kids. You deserve something that makes you happy too."

"Thank you," she breathed. "This is just too much."

"For all you've done, it can never be enough," Patrick replied.

A few minutes later, everyone entered the party room for the slide show. As Emily sat watching, she thought about how amazing her mom really was. She had collected photos of every one of her friends, at various ages and at various events, throughout the years. Even Julie was well represented. Most of the action photography and sports shots had been taken by Susan herself. Her mom truly had a heart of gold.

Of course, Dad was right. By the time the show concluded, Emily's eyes were red from crying. So were just about everyone else's. Patrick turned the lights on again, looked around at the faces, and said, "It looks like this is a perfect time for some cake!"

Everyone laughed and filtered back out of the room. As Emily was about to leave, Peter approached her from behind, gently grabbed her hand, and pulled her against the far wall. He turned the lights off so that only the glow of the projector softly lit the room.

"I'm seriously thinking that cake can wait for a minute," he murmured when they were alone. He put his arms around her and bent his head down until his lips softly met hers. When he pulled away,

Emily placed her head on his chest and melted completely into him. She was so happy that they had finally surrendered to their undeniable attraction at prom. Since that night, wrapped in his arms was her favorite place to be.

They stayed there, in comfortable silence, until they were interrupted by two words, coming from Jake's talker: "Come on!" Unaware that he had intruded on an intimate moment, he repeated, "Come on! Come on! Come on!"

Jake was beyond himself with excitement and he greedily grabbed one of Emily's hands and one of Peter's. He practically dragged them both to the center of the dance area just as the DJ started playing "Celebration."

Robert, EJ, Warren, Julie, Nat, Sophie, Peter, and Emily encircled Jake as they jumped, danced, and sang. Looking at his face, everyone could see that, in this moment, Jake was in his happy place. Tonight, Emily had to admit, she was right there with him.

Epilogue

They heard her phone ringing as Emily was unlocking the door to her dorm room. It was her mom's ringtone, which was not surprising, since she always FaceTimed on Sunday evening. Emily and her mom spoke or texted multiple times a week, but on Sundays she got to talk to Jake too. That was always an adventure. Having lived with him for his entire life, Emily didn't realize how much she'd come to rely on so many physical aspects of his communication to understand him. Some of those didn't translate as clearly on FaceTime, but they were navigating their way around it and making it work.

She picked up the call on her iPad so she would be able to see them on a larger screen. She was hoping for some good news today. "Hey, Mom!" Emily said.

"Hi, baby!" Susan replied. "It's so good to see your face!"

"Mom, it's only been a week since we FaceTimed, and I just talked to you yesterday!" Emily laughed.

"I know," Susan admitted, "but so much has happened this week that it feels like a lifetime."

"Does that mean you're in?" Emily asked hopefully.

"Yes!" Susan replied. "We moved in on Thursday. We're still getting settled, but let me show you around while I have you here."

They had been making steady progress on the new house ever since they broke ground in April. Even though Emily was only an hour and a half away, she hadn't seen it since she had moved away in mid-August. Cross-country and school were taking up way too much of her time, in this first semester, to even think about a short road trip home. She really missed everyone.

"OK!" Emily responded. "Hold on one second, though. I'm going to move the iPad so we both can see you." Emily set the iPad farther away in order to widen the screen a little.

"Hey, Ms. P!" Peter said when he came into view. "This is such amazing news! I'm so happy for you!"

"Hi, Peter," Susan said. "How are classes going for you?"

"Ehhh...we can talk about that later," Peter said with a grin. "Let's get to the grand tour!"

Susan turned the screen around and showed them the entire house, from the beautiful new kitchen, to the great room, to their new bedrooms, which were practically empty. It wasn't exactly what they had lost, but they were lucky to have a place to call home again.

"I saved the best for last," Susan said with a bright smile as she took them down some stairs. "This is the only place in the house, besides Jake's bedroom, where everything has been unpacked and set up."

When Susan reached the base of the stairs, she revealed a beautiful, brightly painted room with soft carpets, toys, instruments, swings, and a large open space. It was Jake's sensory room. Emily gasped at the sight of it. Susan was obviously very proud of it, and she spoke, in great detail, about everything that had been included and how it would help Jake. As she described its features, Emily and Peter could hear music in the background. It wasn't very good, but it was the unmistakable sound of guitar music. Peter would know that sound anywhere.

"Ms. P, where is that music coming from?" Peter asked with genuine curiosity.

"Don't worry, Peter, we could *never* replace you," Susan replied. "But we did find a pretty cool temporary substitute. He volunteered for the position when he found out that you were leaving. He's a relative newcomer in guitar-playing circles, but maybe you've heard of him. Let me introduce you to…" Susan's voice trailed off for a moment as she turned the screen around. "Mr. Patrick Prescott."

Peter and Emily looked at each other and laughed. Not only had Patrick learned the basics of playing guitar, he was also trying to teach Jake. The two of them sat together in the most comfortable-looking rocking chair Emily had ever seen. Jake was sitting on Patrick's lap. Patrick's large arms encircled Jake and held the guitar as he played. It was the sweetest thing Emily had ever seen in her life. She found herself wishing that the next few weeks would fly by so she could be with her family again. She yearned to finally be home.

About Jake's "Talker"

In *Nonverbal*, Jake uses many forms of communication that do not include words. Among these are sign language, facial expression, noises (called "vocalizations"), leading, gestures, and a communication device. Together, these types of communication are called *augmentative communication* because they augment or enhance spoken language. In Jake's case, his augmentative communication device, or "talker," is an iPad with a communication application. He is able to use the app, by touching picture symbols of words, to create phrases and sentences. This allows him to convey ideas he cannot say clearly. His device then speaks the phrases to his communication partners.

There are many reasons why people use augmentative communication devices. Although Jake's speech difficulties are not specifically named in the book, aspects of two speech disorders are implied. One is called dysarthria of speech, which is a speech disorder that occurs when there is muscle weakness or differences in muscle tone throughout the mouth. The other is called apraxia of speech; it is a neurological disorder that can occur in people with and without Down syndrome. Apraxia of speech is also referred to as a motor planning disorder. Although Jake knows the words he wants to say, he can't translate the plans in his brain into the correct speech movements. This is why, throughout the text, you see people helping him to shape his mouth to make words.

For more information regarding augmentative and alternative communication, dysarthria of speech, or apraxia of speech, please visit asha.org or apraxia-kids.org.

What is Down Syndrome?

Down syndrome, by definition, is a genetic disorder that occurs when a person has an extra copy of the chromosome 21. This is why it is also called "trisomy 21". According to the National Down Syndrome Society (Ndss.org), approximately one in every 700 babies in the United Sates are born with Down syndrome each year. The physical characteristics and development of individuals with Down syndrome are impacted in many similar ways, but there are a wide variety of skills and challenges associated with the diagnosis. Because each individual is unique, I have asked parents of children with Down syndrome to share their personal views to answer the question "What is Down Syndrome?" Below are their responses.

"Down syndrome is the never-ending excitement of seeing something for the first time over and over again. It is getting excited about something you have done 100 times, but it's brand new every time. Down Syndrome is innocent. Down Syndrome is a world of wonder. Down Syndrome is home."

K. D.

"My son with Down Syndrome enjoys a life just as amazing, scary, complicated, beautiful, inspiring, hopeful and unique as anyone else in this world. His journey proves over and over again that we really are all more alike than different."

S. W.

"Having to work harder than other people, even for the smallest task. Never resenting the struggle, but embracing it."

B. H.

"An amazing and unlimited capacity to love and forgive."

M. H.

"Down syndrome is learning to see, hear, experience, and love life in a whole new way."

T.H.

"If you ask me what Down syndrome is, so many thoughts swirl around my head. Almost everyone on the outside believes that people with Down syndrome are always happy and easy going. While that is true some of the time, people with Down syndrome are so much more. They are more alike than different. People with Down syndrome just want to be accepted, have friends, (have) meaningful relationships, lead productive lives and yes....be happy."

E.H.

Acknowledgments

First and foremost, I would like to acknowledge the true inspiration for this book: all of the children I have had the pleasure of working with over the past twenty years. Jake is a combination of many of your most inspiring qualities and characteristics. You have taught me well throughout the years.

I would like to recognize Amy B. McCoy for her feedback regarding the story from its infancy and, also, for her constant encouragement. It means more than you know.

I would like to thank my beta readers and good friends: Bridget Kudla, Sabena Escott, Tamara Buonocore-Hay, Joni Baldwin, and Julie Hodgson. Thank you for looking at this story through each of your individual lenses. Your feedback is very important and deeply appreciated.

Thank you to all of the parents who provided quotes to enlighten us about what Down syndrome is to them. You are the only ones who can truly and personally understand.

Finally, I would like to thank God for his grace. I rely on it every moment of every day.

Made in the USA
Middletown, DE
20 January 2020

83418877R00146